Bears in the Wild

Hot & Hairy Fiction

Bears in the Wild

Hot & Hairy Fiction

Edited by R. Jackson

Volume 3 of the Bearotica series

Bear Bones Books
New London, Connecticut, USA

Bear Bones Books
An imprint of Lethe Press, 118 Heritage Avenue, Maple Shade, NJ 08052
BearBonesBooks.com / lethepressbooks.com / lethepress@aol.com

Printed in the United States of America.

Bears in the Wild: Hot & Hairy Fiction
Edited by R. Jackson

First Edition

Cover photograph of *Jack Radcliffe* by Chris Komater. Used by permission.
Cover design by Niki Smith
Book Design by Toby Johnson

1-59021-245-2 / 978-1-59021-245-5

Contents

Fur-runners

Lewis Merrick

The people kept their distance from me in the little town. In their eyes I was a foreigner, a *fur-runner,* as they pronounce it. Fine with me. I came there to write, and I was perfectly happy not to be disturbed. Behind my back they called me Bear Man because I lived so deep in the woods and because I'm so hairy. You get to my cabin (it's owned by a friend who hasn't been there in years) by going up a road that starts in gravel and turns to dirt and then ends when the trees get too dense to drive through. And even then it's a hike over a ridge before you get to the door. No electricity. A well with a hand pump for water. The only illumination is from the stars and an oil lamp, which cast just enough light over my notebook so I can write through the night.

Bear Man. They can call me what they want. I know they're curious and maybe a little afraid. I'm big — six four or so — and the years of working out have made me sturdy. And their curiosity was piqued even more when Marco showed up. He's a friend from New York, a big Italian guy with as much hair as I have and dark Sicilian looks. Marco was a model, but now he runs one of the top agencies. He discovered Beta Knight, kept her off drugs and placed her on the covers of every fashion magazine in the world. He's a fur-runner, too, and I love when he runs his fur against mine and his big sausage of a dick up my ass.

The townspeople smile, of course, whenever I go by. They say how-do. In the church, they move over so I can take a seat in the pews. But in the back of their minds they'd like to run me out. But I wasn't going to leave until I finished this book — my publisher was breathing down my neck —

and I could only finish it when I was free of all distractions. Marco, well, Marco was only there for a week.

I wrote to Marco to meet me at Martha's Diner because he'd never find my place by himself. Martha's Diner is the only place to eat in town. Martha makes her own pies and the chicken is so fresh you'd think that she'd just grabbed it from the coop. The coffee is rich and thick and gives me a good kick.

I was sitting in the diner waiting for Marco, and Wally was serving me. He's Martha's son. She owns the place. I don't know what happened to Martha's husband, but I never saw a sign of him. Wally helps his mom usually in the kitchen, but sometime at the tables. He's just out of high school, and he's going to the state college on scholarship, "and get out of here," he once told me in a whisper. Wally whispers to me even if no one is in the diner. He's the only one who speaks to me in the entire town. Sometimes he even sits down at my table, the glass coffee carafe in his hand.

I know why he's nervous talking to me even if he doesn't. Wally is an all-American boy, six foot — but not willowy — with coarse blond hair naturally screwed into tight curls and an amazing peaches and cream complexion. The smile, so shy with me, grows dazzling when one of the high school girls comes in asking for something. It's clear that he's popular, and he talks to them in an easy, open way. I can tell, even if they can't, that there isn't the slightest desire in his voice because I've heard that desire, gurgling ever so softly behind his whisper.

He's queer all right. I can tell it from the way he looks at me, as if he would like to dive into my eyes and swim inside. Or maybe wrestle me to the ground until I mastered him. He'd want to lose.

But if he had it bad for me, it was almost comic what happened when Marco came through the door. From my window, I could see Marco get out of the rented car and swagger up the short walk (he's retained that rolling gait he learned as a runway model), his $300 t-shirt pulled tight against his body and his nipples — those extraordinary volcanic cones — jutting out. His chest hair rolled over the collar like a little ruff. The loose jeans were cut in such a way that when he walked they showed the enormous length of his dick. He looked straight ahead with those mirrored insect-looking glasses that I hate to see him wear because they hide his eyes, which are as sharp as two arrows headed straight through your heart.

I watched Marco walk into the diner, but Wally only saw him when the little bell at the front door tinkled. The kid nearly dropped the carafe he was holding on his way to giving me a warm up. He was paralyzed. Then his jaw dropped, and his cock pushed out from his boxers. Marco looked him over and then saw me waving to him from the corner.

"Hey, buddy!" I stood up and we embraced, then he kissed me on both cheeks so he could whisper, "What's with the kid?" into my ear. "Tell you later," I answered.

Marco sat down. It took awhile for Wally to gather his sense and grab the dirty little-used menu. But he was still unaware of the rod he'd thrown in his pants. He stood next to Marco and turned to give him the menu.

"Hey, kid, don't poke me in the eye with that thing," Marco laughed and put his hand on the bulge to push it away.

"Oh, God," Wally groaned, and ran back into the kitchen.

Marco leaned over to me, "I do believe I made the kid come."

"Why not?" I answered. "You always make me come."

"But not after only one touch."

"Well, I'm not eighteen, and I bet that's the first time any guy ever touched his hard dick."

"I'd guess that it was the first time anyone ever touched his hard dick." Marco looked over the menu, then flipped it aside. "What's good? I've been travelling all day to get here."

"The chicken's always fine."

"Chicken it is."

And with that Wally returned to take our orders, an apron now covering the front of his pants.

I'd already been staying in the cabin a few months, and once I got Marco back there, I was almost as ready to shoot as Wally.

"I'd like to rip those clothes off you," I told him.

"Well, why don't you."

And I took my teeth and yanked the t-shirt off and with it a hair or two. Marco yowled with his telling mixture of pain and delight. The jeans, already loose, got pulled off with one yank, and there he was naked on the mattress on the floor. The body was perfect — only it was manlier than ever, shaggy with hair. His dick looked like a missile ready for launching, but it could wait. What I wanted were his big heavy balls. They looked like those sacks in pirate movies filled with doubloons; only these were filled with something even more precious.

Once down at his balls, I could get the rich, musty smell of his manhood (I wouldn't allow him to shower for at least two days) and I began to get some spit on his ass. He grabbed his legs so I could pull his crack open. There was hair almost up to the little anus with its pink lips that needed pulling apart, a finger or two to explore inside. I couldn't so much hear as feel the hum of pleasure coming from Marco's throat.

He reached for his pants and pulled out a condom.

"No more preliminaries? We have all week."

"I haven't had it in months. Not since you left. And I don't want to wait anymore."

He didn't have to say more. In seconds the sheath was rolled down my not unsubstantial dick and covered with great gobs of spit. Another gob on his asshole, and I rested the head of my dick on that pretty ring that glowed in the light of the lantern.

I knew Marco likes it rough, but I wanted to tease him. I pressed down with only the slightest pressure, and I could feel that portal giving way. He was that hungry. But I went no further. I heard a little moan, and then I felt his fingers on the back of my legs pulling me toward him. He moved his butt a little toward me, and my dickhead went in just a little more. He tried again to move toward me, and I moved away.

"Shhh," I whispered. "Shhh."

He let go of my thigh. He relaxed. I was in charge. And then I pushed forward with all my might.

"Aaaagh," he cried in surprise and with the intense combination of pain and delight.

"Aaaagh," I heard, and the second cry comingled desire and despair.

But the sound didn't come from Marco. It was from someone outside our window.

In an instant we were both on our feet running outside. We couldn't see very much — there was only a quarter moon — but there was enough that we could make out the person ahead of us. The guy was fast, whoever he was, and the stones were rough on my bare feet.

He was over the ridge, and I could see that he was heading for a pick-up parked beside ours. He was opening the door, but at that moment, his pants slid down to his thighs, and he was tangled up in them. He reached down with his right hand to pull them up, but it gave me just enough time to grab it and pull the arm back. He tried to push me off, but I was stronger and soon got the other arm, and I yanked the two high so there'd be some pain.

Marco was at my side. He brought some ropes that we had been planning to use for other purposes, and tied the guy's arms and then his kicking legs. We carried the peeping tom back to the cabin, but by then he had given up fighting. He swung between us like a bagged deer.

"What do you plan to do to him?" Marco asked as we walked through the woods. I was sure he had ideas of his own.

"Something he won't forget," I answered.

Then Marco and I were silent, and the man between us breathed rapidly with fear.

We swung the door open and hauled him in feet first. The lantern light now revealed who it was.

"Wally!" I exclaimed, in mock surprise, because I had guessed who the perpetrator was midway in our race to the car. "Wally, what are you doing here?"

"It was so beautiful," he said.

" 'It'? '*It*'? What do you mean by 'it'?"

"What you were doing, it was so beautiful. I knew it would be. The two of you are so ... so beyond anything I've ever seen here. And I could tell you were more than friends, even before he touched my prick. Did you know I came when he touched me?"

"I had a pretty good idea," Marco told him, and Wally blushed.

"I don't know what came over me. As soon as you guys left I called my Mom and asked her to take over at the diner so I could follow you. I didn't mean any harm. I had no idea what I was going to do, but I wanted to talk to you. I wanted to see you. And it was beautiful."

"It is beautiful, and so are you," Marco said with that voice that I knew would melt him.

"You think I am?"

"Yes, I do?"

"But I'm not big like you two guys."

"Well, I don't know," I said, and I reached into his pants and pulled out his dick, and in a few seconds, as I rolled it with my thumb, it came fully alive. It was much longer than I thought it would be, and a lot, lot thicker. "Believe me, you're big enough to suit any guy," and I bent over to kiss him. His lips were soft and warm, and they parted so I could get my tongue between them. Then Marco went down to get his bit of sugar while I began sucking the boy's dick.

In no time the bindings were down. Not just the ropes around Wally's hands and feet, but the bindings on his psyche. He couldn't wait to get his first taste of cock, and he took to dick like a rabbit takes to lettuce.

All of a sudden, I wanted Wally's dick in me. "Fuck me," I told him.

He looked up uncertain and turned to Marco as if asking permission.

"Go ahead, kid, you heard the man," Marco told him.

"But I ... but I ..."

"No *buts* about it, boy," Marco growled. "It won't hurt him, I promise you. I've been there before hundreds of times. And Marco reached into his pants for one more of his endless supplies of condoms, and ripped one open, and placed it over Wally's dick with his mouth. He'd also found a bottle of lubricant.

Marco sat on my face so he could hold my legs in the air and give Wally an unimpeded view of the target. "All right down there?" Marco jokingly asked me, as he held my legs beneath his armpits so he could spread the cheeks of my ass. He gave my hole a few drops of lubricant and then swathed a good deal more around Wally's cock, which he positioned at the entrance.

"I like it rough," Marco told him, "but this one likes it slow."

Wally pushed in, and Marco told me later he thought the boy would faint. All I could see (and smell) was Marco's furry ass. Wally didn't know how to control his speed — he'd learn that quickly in the next few days — so after a few inches of slow glide there was an accelerated pace until his entire cock was in me and his balls pummeled my ass.

Once Wally was safely in, Marco got up so I could watch the boy's face. Wally's eyes were closed. But every once in a while they would flicker open, and when he saw me smiling at him, he would give me an extra strong thrust.

Marco was standing behind Wally, admiring the kid's ass, watching the muscles clearly etched beneath the young man's skin. Marco knelt and caressed Wally's ass, and I saw Wally's eyes open with a kind of ecstasy that I've only seen in baroque religious paintings. I couldn't hold it in. Rivers of built up jism flew through the air, lacy white ribbons, some reaching past my shoulder, one hitting Wally right in the chest. It was then that he gave his animal cry and spent time after time into my ass, while Marco let shoot his load over Wally and me.

Wally then collapsed on top of me, and Marco lay on top of Wally.

We rested.

It wasn't going to be long, I knew, before we would be at the games again.

Marco got up first. He had to pee, and while he was out Wally asked, "Do you think Marco would fuck me?"

"The question, Wally, is whether you're ready to be fucked by Marco."

"I am, I am. I dream about getting fucked and sometimes when I beat off. ..." He stopped, unsure whether to continue.

"How many fingers have you gotten into your ass?"

"All of them."

"Come on. The truth."

"Well, four at one time. Is that enough?"

"I think four is sufficient, but this is going to be different."

"I want it to be different. I want it to give me a lot more pleasure, and a bit more pain."

"You've got it."

And as if on cue, Marco returned to the cabin. His dick even when limp was a threatening instrument, hanging down heavily like a club.

"Wally wants to be fucked, Marco, and he wants you to fuck him."

"He does?" Marco asked, but it was less of a question than a statement.

"I do," Wally replied in a strangely small voice.

Marco had bent down and planted a big kiss on Wally's face, "You're going to have great time. Don't worry, I've done this before."

I knew where Marco kept his cash of condoms, and I already had the lubricant. Wally took my hand.

"It's going to be all right, son." I told him, "I'm going to be here right next to you."

"I'd like you to be in me, too," he said softly.

"They'll be time for that," I told him.

Marco had rolled a pillow under Wally's ass and another behind his head, which rested in my arms. I held Wally's hand and leaned over so I could alternately kiss and whisper into his ear, "You've got the greatest ass … Marco's going to make it feel special … you're beautiful … just lay back … let Marco do all the work. …"

Marco had his wedge-like dick at the glorious aperture, and he looked into Wally's eyes like Svengali, getting him to relax, to open up. Marco watched Wally's breathing, and with microscopic degrees eased himself into that anteroom of anal pleasure, waiting for the big doors to give way. And they did. Just a crack at first. Marco advanced slowly until a twinge of pain went through Wally's body, and then made a tactical withdrawal. Wally gripped my hand. And I began my mantra again: "You've got the greatest ass … Marco's going to make it feel special … you're beautiful … just relax … let Marco do all the work."

And then, in what we knew was only a momentary surrender, the sphincter seemed to welcome Marco's dick, and Marco went slowly in. The doors tried to close again, but it was too late. They had relented. Wally breathed the gasp of amazement, the gasp of being filled with another man, the gasp of complete surrender to sensation.

Marco lowered himself and kissed Wally, then me. We all three kissed, and then slowly he began the rhythmic motion of a violin bow gliding across the strings of nerves. Sometimes Marco would play only on one string lightly, but sometime he pressed down hard, make all the strings vibrate together.

Wally was quiet at first, but then he, like a Stradivarius, let out a low growl that got progressively higher as Marco worked the boy's ass faster and harder. And then Wally reached a note that only dogs — if any were close enough — could hear. It was a note that seemed to get stuck in Wally's throat and after a short diversion squirted from his dick. A string of opals fell across his stomach and chest. It was too much for Marco, who blew his own load into the boy's butt. And I, with the one hand free, brought myself to climax that seemed to go on and on like something out of Wagner.

From then on Wally came by our cabin every night for a little learning and lubricant. During the day Marco told me of his plans. Sex-a-faction was about to come out with a new men's line and they needed a face no one had seen before and that would appeal to young men (and older ones as well). He thought Wally could be that face. He told Wally his idea, and at first Wally was scared and overwhelmed. But soon he got used to the idea. He'd be under Marco's care, and if it didn't work out, he could start school in the spring.

It did work out. Wally — now renamed Peter Ferris for his iron dick — was the face of Sex-a-faction for many years. He went to school, even got a degree in fashion and joined Marco's company as a partner. Of course, he was also Marco's partner outside of the office. The two are inseparable. But every now and then they let me come between them, or in them.

As for that book, I got it done, and after a couple of years, it's been optioned by a major studio. I'm now writing the screenplay. That's why I'm back at the cabin, trying to avoid all distraction, happy again to be a fur-runner.

Lewis Merrick *makes his home in the back hills of Tennessee, where he makes a living carving ducks.*

Pueblo Harley Biker

Otto Stahl

Dip dots are little round insignia badges that Harley-Davidson motorcycle dealers sell, each marked with the name of the dealership. I have a buddy, a motorcycle cop, who collects them. So, anytime I travel, I try to find Harley dealers.

The clerk at the gas station had said that I couldn't miss the Pueblo Harley-Davidson dealership, that I'd see the bright orange roof from the freeway. She was right — the roof was like a beacon.

I pulled in and backed my camper van into a parking space against the tan, gravelly hillside. As I walked toward the showroom, it was hard to ignore the argument that swirled like a dust storm in front of the service entrance. Two men stood toe-to-toe. The man facing me was the shorter of the two, with a Mohawk haircut and a very handsome face. The bald man facing away from me had "Brotherhood Cheyenne" across the back of his jacket and was about six and a half feet tall. Both men had plenty of work-hardened muscles.

Just as I opened the door for the parts department, the older one shouted: "Fuck you. Here's your shit. I'm going on to Jicarilla." I looked back through the tinted glass door in time to see him poke the younger one in the chest with a thick finger.

"Lover's quarrel?" I said jokingly to the woman behind the counter.

"Nope, oil-and-gas field workers. Always boom and bust. His bike came in last night on a flatbed tow truck, and he still owes the driver twenty bucks for that. He'll probably try to sell us his bike less the cost of repairs and the tow. So what can I do for you, handsome?" she replied, with a tired, seen-it-all look on her face.

I bought a dip dot and went back outside. I didn't see either of the men until I rounded the front porch. Mohawk man was pacing in the shade of the front porch. He turned, saw me, and stopped short. Fuck, he was handsome. His weather-hardened face had made him look older, and now I realized that he was only in his early twenties.

Looking right into his eyes, I asked him, "Do you like your bike?"

"Yes," he grunted, looking at me like I was an idiot.

"Do you want to sell it to the dealer? They won't give you much."

"No," another grunt.

"What are you going to do?"

"I don't know," he replied in a totally forlorn voice.

I visually sized him up again, trying to reassure myself that I could end anything I was about to start, then said, "Let me make you an offer. I'll pay for what you owe now, give you a place to stay, feed you, and pay for the repairs on your bike." I paused, and locked my gaze on his face, which showed a glimmer of hope. "In return, I ride every hole you've got, any way I want, as long as I want, as hard as I want, and as often as I want until your bike is fixed. If you want to take me up on my offer, get into my camper and get naked. If I like what I see and feel, then we have a deal."

After giving me a cold, hard, murderous look, he dropped his head and mumbled, "I'm not …," then turned on his heels and walked away. He sat on the edge of the porch and stared at his boots.

I climbed into the driver's seat and waited a few moments. He sat there like a rock, expression unchanged. I didn't think he'd go for it.

Turning the key, I started the motor, put it into gear, and headed down the drive. He leapt out in front of me so suddenly I had to slam on the brakes. He walked to the driver's side window. "Alright," was all he said. "Alright what?" I asked. "Alright, I'll do it … *Sir*," he slowly replied through almost-clenched teeth.

I backed up into a parking space against the hill with him jogging along side. I leaned out the window and said, "Walk in the back door, don't say a word, take all your clothes off, and do what you're told."

The camper's rear door had barely closed as his leather motorcycle jacket, snap-button cowboy shirt, A-shirt, boots, leather chaps, worn blue jeans, and torn white jockstrap all hit the floor in rapid succession. He didn't waste any time stripping off, which I took to mean he had committed mentally to the idea. He was slab of labor-made muscle from head to toe.

"Turn around. Spread your legs and arms. Put your jockstrap back on. Turn around again." I said. *Hell yes, he'll do,* I thought to myself. Unlike the uniform crop of jet black fur that covered me from brush cut to toe knuckles, the hair on his body gradated from the dark red, almost brown of his mohawk, to a coppery red on his chest, red blonde at his crotch bush, and finally just blond down his hairy legs. He had my favorite kind of happy trail — a triangle of hair in the small of his back that pointed down to the crack of his fuzzy bubble butt.

"Get on your knees." Yanking down my zipper, I walked over to him, fishing my cock out of my left pants leg as I approached. His look turned to fear. "Suck on this," I said, putting the egg-sized head of my cock to his lips. He reached up and wrapped both hands around the shaft, one above the other, like gripping a baseball bat, and tentatively, delicately licked around the thick ring of my foreskin. "Put your tongue inside. Move it around, I want to feel it." His tongue slipped between my cockhead and foreskin and I could feel my shaft go from hard to rock hard as his tongue darted across the sensitive underside of my prick. "Good, now open up," I said, shoving the head of my cock into his mouth, forcing him to open wide. "Keep that tongue moving and suck on it." He jacked my shaft with both his hands, and squirmed away if I shoved in more than the tip, which just pissed me off. Grabbing his mohawk, I yanked him backward off my cock and leaned down and got in his face.

"Where did you learn to suck cock like that?" I barked at him, an inch from his face.

"Oklahoma State Reform School," he answered sheepishly.

"Good, then I know exactly how to help you focus. Put your forehead on the floor, and your hands behind your back." I dug around in the overhead compartment until I found what I was looking for. After clicking a pair of handcuffs closed around his wrists, I pulled his head back up to my groin. Putting my hand under his chin, I slipped my thumb into his mouth. He looked up at me with lost puppy eyes. "If you want my help, don't suck my cock like some priss who thinks it is nasty. Get into it. No hands and no tooth marks. Lick everything, get it good and slick, because it is all going down your throat."

Taking him by the ear, I guided his mouth on a tour of my crotch. "That's it, lick my balls." Rocking my hips, I drew my cock down along his lips in a long stroke that ended with the head of my cock cupped in his outstretched tongue. "You know what to do here, stick your tongue back inside the foreskin and lick around. Good." Turning my hips, I shifted so that his tongue glided down the left side of my cock. "Suck that ball, see if you can get it in your mouth," I said as I tucked the last of my left nut into his mouth. "Nice, suck hard." I got a rush as the heat from his mouth and suction pressure enveloped my nut. "Now the other one," I said, moving his head to the other side. My dick stretched past the side of his head, and drooled a silvery thread of precum down the back of his neck as he worked on my balls.

Letting go of his ear, I put my hands behind my back, and stood at attention. I twitched my dick in his face. Much to my surprise, he lunged forward and kept licking along my balls and shaft, as high as he could reach. I expected him to stop the second I let go of him. Looking down, I put my thumb on top of my shaft and pressed down hard so it pointed right into his mouth. I don't know what surprised me more: the way he pounced on my cock, sucking hard while his tongue skated around, or that his newly hard prick poked awkwardly out of his frayed jockstrap.

I ran the fingertips of my hands along the ridge of his mohawk haircut. The total feeling was very sensuous, the stiff yet silky hair brushed through my fingers in contrast to the hard, scratchy warmth of his shaven skull under my palms, and the warm wet suction surrounding my cock head. "Take a deep breath," I said. He looked up at me with a mixture of fear and desire, and I felt a rush of cool air across my dick as he breathed in through his nose. Bringing my hands together behind his head, I interlaced my fingers to hold him in place. Driving my pelvis forward, I felt his momentary hesitation as he gagged on my cock as it hit the top of his throat. His throat, fighting hard to spit me out, felt like hundreds of tiny fingers massaging my dick. I tilted his head a bit, feeling for the right place, and then thrust deeply into his throat. Popping through the oval of sphincter muscle in his throat electrified my whole body, and I felt my shaft flare and swell inside him. He looked up at me in fear, gyrating to try and get off my cock. I tightened my grip on his head and mashed his face into my crotch as he struggled. His nose was finally buried in my thick pubes and I felt the stubble on his chin against my balls. Pleasure surged through me. I pulled out and slapped him hard across the face with my cock to get him refocused. "Swallow all that spit and take another deep breath."

I like to watch my cock slide in and out of a man, so when I pulled out, I could see his dick twitching — and noticed that the rougher I handled him, the harder his dick twitched. His cock didn't angle like mine, but stuck straight out from his body, and looked hard enough to pound nails with.

Putting my cock back in his mouth, I widened my stance and moved forward so that my legs straddled his torso. The hardness of his musculature, the warmth of his skin and the undulations of his rib cage felt good between my legs. The front of my hairy thighs were against his smooth, hard biceps, forcing his handcuffed arms back, levering his head down onto me like he's bobbing for apples.

Determined to remake him, I alternated long, deep, slow inch-at-a-time strokes with fast, furious ones that popped my sensitive dickhead in and out of his throat. He was one of those guys who could never say that he needed to serve a man, but his boner spoke for him. Just when I thought he would either bite my dick or pass out from lack of air, I would pull back but only far enough for him to steal a partial breath, and then slam back in. Soon he was a gasping, trembling, drooling, sweaty mess from the effort of accommodating my long, thick crank, but he no longer resisted my invasion. I couldn't remember the last time my cock had felt slipperier, warmer, or more at home.

Holding him in place, I quickly sawed four or five deep strokes into him. I loved the feeling of the slick, soft and tight squeeze as I entered his throat. Deep-throat spit dripped down my shaft and off my balls. Rising up on my toes, I grabbed the back of his head, and snapped my hips forward, and sank home into his throat, deep-dicking him until his nose was hidden in my pubes and my balls scraped against his chin. Using a combination of moving his head back and forth, and rocking my hips, I pulled out until his pursed lips just kissed my piss slit, then drove back into him until those same lips were stretched wider than I'm sure he thought they could be, firmly sealed around the base of my fat cock. In each of the moments of stillness when I was as deep in his throat as could be, he struggled intensely not to gag, to breathe, to pull himself off me, and to swallow or spit out the ocean of saliva and precum that flooded him.

Dozens of strokes later I stepped back, and he almost toppled over, everything but his rigid dick exhausted. He was trying to breathe, swallow, and compose himself all at the same time. His body slumped forward, and his chin was on his chest. I held my cock in one hand, and picked up his bowed head by his Mohawk, like a battlefield trophy, with my free hand. He turned his eyes up toward me, unsure. I blew my heavy load all over his handsome face, then used my cock to smear my cum around as it dripped down his face, until my over-sensitized cock couldn't take his stubble any more. The thick, ropy heaviness of my softening cock hung alongside his face as he rested his head on my thigh, still breathing heavily. Nuzzling into my balls, he flicked his tongue out to cleanly catch a pearl of cum seeping out of my dick.

Lots of thoughts swirled around in my head about what to do with him next. I wanted to start training his ass, but that would have to wait.

"Clean it up," I said as I pulled back my foreskin and pressed the meat of my cockhead against his battered lips. Without a fight, he rose a little off his heels and forced himself to swallow down my cock until his nose was again at my pubes. He looked up at me with dick-drunk eyes as he nursed slowly on my softened cock, the resentment gone. I could feel a shiver go down his back as I stroked my hands along his Mohawk, and then used it as a handle to gently pull him off me. "Good boy, but if you get me fired up again, we won't get in there before they close tonight," I said, as my cock slipped slowly from his lips and dropped heavily against my balls.

"Bow down," I said. As soon as I unlocked his handcuffs, his hands flew to his crotch — one hand pulled at his ball sac, the other frenetically stroked his cock. None too gently, I kicked his hands away with my boot toe. "You come when I let you," was all I had to say. Poor fuck, he was so excited that his dick was quivering like a puppy's tail. I had no idea how he was going to get it back into his pants, but that was his problem. "Clean up and get dressed," I said, throwing him a towel. "Let's go make the repair arrangements."

We walked back into the dealership and headed for the service counter. I paid for the rest of the tow, and the diagnostic work. The service manager said it would be three days for the parts to arrive from Milwaukee, and another two to put it all back together. They don't work Sundays. Six days to ride Mohawk man. After the skull-fucking session I'd just had in the parking lot, the cost of repairs was money well spent. As we walked back to the camper, I noticed a tiny bead of my cum glistening on the back of his head and felt my dick stir.

***Otto Stahl** is an ex-Marine musclebear who works as a custom logger in New England. He enjoys training men.*

DUPLEX/COMPLEX

Smith Kendall

Jack says I'm going to suck his cock before the day's over.

I snort.

He smiles and continues to haul boxes down from Ernie's duplex. We have to climb up the one flight up to his posh apartment — hardwood floors, a sun room, a skylight and a working fireplace in the living room, a dining room with its original built-in cabinets and woodwork left intact, a kitchen with a gas range, and two bedrooms.

I knew of Ernie's unfavorable reputation before we shook hands and prepped the creaky steps up to his place and the ramp into our huge van. As much as I don't care for his looks — average build with great furry pecs, nervous eyes, and bad teeth in his forties — I sort of feel sorry for him, actually. Ernie had stepped on far too many toes within the local bear community so some guys stopped going to bear events because they knew he was going to be there. He was apparently so goddamn pushy, hitting on everyone like there was no tomorrow, even on those who he knew were in monogamous relationships *and* in front of their husbands.

Maybe it was because he'd come out two years earlier, after being married to a frigid woman for years, so he felt like the proverbial kid in a candy store, or maybe he thought he needed space from his first and only boyfriend, who really did love him. Either way he hadn't quite understood that acceptance into the bear community, no matter how muscular and furry one might be, doesn't happen overnight. Those things take time. So Ernie slept with the wrong men who proceeded to tell everyone else that Ernie couldn't always get it up, or that he was a very slow riser, or that he was a lousy fuck who happened to think that he was a Dom top.

But really, why does the bear community have to pick on each other like that? Do we really hate each other that much? I say, give the poor fella a chance to grow up. Hell, we've all been teenagers once — no matter how old we are when we come out! So yeah, I'll never get that part of the community, especially those who never understand the need for privacy and respect for one's personal life, but yeah, I have buds here and there. Some I've fucked, but mostly I cherish as friends when I hang out at the Eagle.

Still, I keep my lid shut like I keep all my escapades quiet from my wife; she simply does not care to know who I am fucking as long as it's another man. She cares that she is the *only* woman in my life, and that I was to sleep next to her every night. I love her, and our two children, even more. I used to be a manager at a cereal making plant but thanks to the economy and the banking credit crisis of late, I was laid off. That was how I ended up helping my buddy Jack with his moving company.

Anyway, Jack and I met at one of those bear dances a few years back. A mutual friend introduced us to each other, and we hit it off, talking about movies and shit like that. I didn't feel attracted to him, as he was a bit too beefy for me; well, he had too big of a belly. I know I shouldn't be picky about how people look, but he had deep acne scars around his cheeks that he tried to camouflage with his beard. Under the laser eyes of harsh lighting one could still see through the beard and see the jaggy ridges. He told me once that he'd always felt ugly and fat in high school, so he showed me his mug shot from his senior yearbook. Beardless, he still had a devilish grin. "Shee-it," I said. "You ain't that bad."

He looked at me. "You think I should shave off my beard?"

"God, no. Just be yourself."

He nodded quietly and put away the yearbook.

Over time it became apparent that he was in love with me. This became a real problem because per my agreement with my wife, I was not to do boyfriends. She said that I am a great husband and a better father than any father she knows, but I could never leave her for another man. She couldn't bear it. The fact that my heart was unattainable as a result has inexplicably made me very attractive to a lot of men who get off on the idea of conquering my body *and* my heart. It used to bother me a great deal that men — especially cubs in search of a bear daddy — would think that I could be a father figure to them, but I've learned to get over it and embraced my daddyhood. It was a bit strange to think that my age by itself — I'm in my mid-fifties — could make me that much more sexually desirable, but hey, whatever works to get them into my pants! I get them a good deal more than they realize. The world's full of fathers who don't give a fuck about their children, so these kids, especially if they're gay, grow up seeking the attention and nurturing they never got from their own biological dads. Sometimes I'll role-play as their father and fuck the shit out of these young men who keep screaming for more, and harder. It's truly extraordinary how lovingly these spent puppies look up at me when we're done. "You're a good kid," I always say. Boy, that remark always put a big smile on their faces when I leave. But I hate breaking their hearts when I remind them again: "I don't do boyfriends."

Anyway, Jack's a few years younger than me. He's also a few inches shorter than me, but he's very strong, almost like an ox with a permanent yoke on his shoulders. He's got a droll sense of humor, which cracks me up half the time. He knows that I don't see him as a prospective fuck. Still, he seems to have forgiven me. We go to movies and bear beer busts together on my one night "out with the boys" once a week.

The hauling seems to go on forever and my feet are starting to hurt, but Jack's quips tossed about as we pass each other with boxes, lamps, and whatnot make me chuckle: "I really should de-IKEA-ize my apartment before I move." Or, "Jesus, is this box filled with lead dildos or what?" Or, "Wonder if that big box's got teddy bears that'll grope us to death?" I nearly died laughing over that one because we could see Ernie trying to finish packing the rest of his unorganized shit, but it was all out of his earshot. If he'd overheard us, he might've fired us. It was that funny.

Over lunch we sit on the steps out in front of the building. Cars and people pass us by on this fine October day. The weather's not too cold yet, but it's perfect because we've sweated a lot carrying the stuff all morning so we never feel too hot like we might've in the summer. We wolf down our sandwiches and gulp down our Cokes, but we're pretty quiet, lost in our own thoughts.

"Hey."

"What?"

"Remember what I said earlier today?"

"That" — I glance around to make sure no one was close by to overhear us — "I'm gonna be your cocksucker by day's end?" I shake my head. "Ain't gonna happen. Sorry about that, mate."

"You don't know what I'm really like."

"Let's just stay friends, okay?"

He nods and gets up. "Bathroom," he says and enters the duplex upstairs.

I feel really crappy. I don't like to make my friends feel bad, but after having tried to do a pity fuck with a guy I didn't feel hot for, I swore that I'd never do that again. Too embarrassing to see how my cock could go limp in a minute in front of a hole lubed up and waiting for me to enter when I didn't care for the guy in the first place. Uh-*hunh.*

When he returns, he doesn't look me in the eye. I pull the blankets off the stairs and walk gingerly around the duplex, checking to make sure that there's nothing left to take. Ernie looks at me and says, "I think you guys got everything. I'll meet you over at the other place in a half hour."

"Okay." I turn to leave.

"Is Jack okay?"

"What?"

"I think he was crying."

"Oh," I lie. "I wouldn't know anything about that."

"I made the mistake of hurting my first boyfriend."

I nod. I'd met his first boyfriend long before they hooked up, and I always thought he was a nice guy, a bit energetic when he talked. Just not my type, was all. Still, he had a very fuckable ass. Jack thought so too; he had the hots for him that went nowhere. But the bear grapevine said that he wasn't the type to hook up. He wanted nothing less than a LTR.

"Well. I should get going."

He nods.

After we close up the van, I say, "Want me to drive?"

"No. I know how to get there."

We are quiet as he navigates through the early afternoon traffic. We arrive two neighborhoods away in front of a huge apartment complex. Ernie isn't out in front to let us into the basement garage so Jack turns off the engine and keeps his eyes away from mine.

"I'm sorry —"

"Don't."

"Please. Let me talk."

"I don't want to hear your voice."

I'm about to say, "Oh, man," but I bite my lip.

Ernie finally arrives with his packed car and allows us into the building.

The hauling between van and freight elevator up to the seventh floor is less painful now that we have huge carts. We take turns swapping the carts, rarely looking into each other's eyes. Somehow the tension has forced us to move things a lot more quickly; there's no fun left in our movements. We behave strictly like factory workers, like the men and women I'd used to supervise at the plant.

Two hours later we are done. I stand watch as Jack tears off the signed receipt of delivery services rendered and hands it to Ernie, who then gives me a look that says, "Go talk to him."

I say nothing.

I follow Jack into the cavernous freight elevator. The minute the doors slide shut, I press the WAIT button and pull Jack into my arms and plunge my tongue down his throat. Equally stunned as I am, he grabs me back into his arms and pushes my tongue down my throat, fishes me back into him. I taste the hunger, not realizing how keen a man's senses can become in a time of constant starvation from that ache to have a full-blooded no-holds-barred relationship with a man like I have with my wife. I rub my beard all over his, licking the salt of sweat from his face.

His hands grip my face as he stares up into my eyes. "You're lonely."

I shake my head no.

"You need a *man*, something that only men can give you. It's not the same between a man and a woman."

"I'm not going to leave my wife."

"I'm not saying that you should. Just —"

I grab his head and lick across his lips. I knew exactly what he meant, but I didn't want to hear it.

His hands go wild all over my chest, seeking out the exact location of my nipples through my flannel shirt. Once he feels its twin bumps, he tweaks them a bit.

I moan.

He squeezes them again. Hard.

I grunt.

He's already figured out that my nips are connected to my cock. His stubby fingers apply the right amount of pressure, and the feel of flannel rubbing against my furry chest makes it all delightfully worse.

I respond with my hands pulling up his T-shirt, sluggish with the soak of sweat. The waft of his musk hits my nostrils like a tsunami. How could I have not noticed? I stop him from tossing away his shirt and bring it up to my face. I lick all over its stinky armpit areas and inhale as he watches.

I bring the wet spots of his shirt to his mouth, and together we make love to the sweat that will soon drench us. His tongue licks the salt crystals off the fabric, and I sweep them off him onto my tongue. He grabs my hand and rubs his face all over its back. "Fuck," he says. "I've always loved you because of this thick fur on the back of these hands!"

I chuckle. "Well, that's me."

I hook one of his hands and bring it up to my mouth, sucking each of his five fingers, ending with a loving blow job to his fat, grime-covered thumb. Somehow us sucking each other's fingers and licking each other's hands feels far more intimate than just another 69. We use our hands so much that we often forget what it feels like to have them caressed by another tongue, another mouth.

He unbuttons my flannel shirt and lifts up one of my arms. He zeroes into the dense patch of fur in my armpit. As he licks deeper into the heart of each follicle sopping with sweat, his voice sounds no longer human but the sound of an animal devouring its prey after a long winter's hunt. He is pure carnal. His fingers never leave my nipples as he switches to my other armpit. My armpits are so thick that I don't feel ticklish at all; they're almost like Brillo pads.

I stop him and bring his face to mine. I dive into his mouth for the taste of my own armpit sweat; yes, this is what being *male* is all about, being unafraid of one's own sweat and sharing it with another who understands completely what it means to be a man, growing up and wondering whether one was masculine enough while learning the language of one's body's own hot spots, all so easy to master when our body parts are so similar.

I lick all over the remnants of his adolescent acne on his face and return to our tongue wrestling.

He pushes me against the blanketed wall of the elevator, holds up my arms, and dives into the sea of fur surrounding my nipples. "Fuck," I whisper. He sure knows how to torture, licking me not just broadly but with varying pressures here and there. It's almost as if he knows that each square inch of my chest has its own nerve endings waiting for tender stimulation as this, his tongue, his eyes drinking me in from above as I try not to buckle under the weight of his loving attentions.

Then he nibbles my aching nips.

It is then I almost cream in my jeans.

"Jack, Jack ...." I put my hand up to block his extraordinary tongue.

"What?"

"I don't want to come just yet."

"I'm that good, huh?" He grins.

I kiss him on the forehead.

He unbuckles his jeans and pushes it down once he kicks off his sneakers. A huge continent of precum has soaked his frayed jockstrap. He knows I love exhibitionists, so he grips his sizable erection rather proudly. He grins again.

I take off the rest of my clothes. My uncut cock bobs up, slapping my belly rather loudly when I pull off my underwear.

We stand there, naked and staring at each other in a moment of hunger.

"I don't know why —" I start.

He puts his finger up to his lips. "Later." He lifts his arms and licks at his own armpits. I had no idea that his tongue was that long.

"Fuck," I say. "That's so hot."

"What are you waiting for? Come join me."

I plunge into his rank aromas. Nights of standing next to him in the bar — not knowing what a bundle of incredible treasures his body held there inside a T-shirt and ill-fitting jeans — imploded in my own body. I had to taste more.

Without further ado, I drop to my knees, spin him around, and pull apart his furry asscheeks. There, the center of his asshole winked. I brought my nose right up to it, inhaling the unearthly scent sucking my tongue inside him. I pressed against the puckered insides of him, and again when I felt his sphincter muscles opening and closing. *Fuck,* I thought. *He must know how to really take care of a man's cock up his ass.*

I stand up and stick out my tongue, offering the taste of his ass. He devours my tongue as my uncut cock juts up against his furry belly. He strokes my thick cock, slow and easy, with an occasional tug at its foreskin, as we trade slurps. Then he begins to work my nips again.

I drop my hand down to his crotch and feel the throbbing contours of his cock. His jockstrap is soaking wet.

I get down on my knees and push him against the wall. He raises his arms gladly, and as I spit all over his pouch and lick all over his shaft through the very thin fabric, I hear him grunt and slurp all over his own armpits.

I smell the dried piss and cum and sweat in his jockstrap. This gives me an idea. "Hey, Jack? You like piss?"

"Hell yeah! Thought you'd never ask."

"You got it coming."

I massage my cock a bit to soften it enough to unleash my bladder. I chuckle at his saucer-wide eyes when he sees how I can piss through my hard-on.

"Oh, fuck! I'm gonna come!"

I grab his cock at the tip. "Don't." I continue squirting my piss all over his crotch and thighs. "I want you to fuck me."

"Fuck shit oh *shit*."

But it's too late. He rocks uncontrollably in my hand as his pouch sags with a mouthful's worth of cum and then some. His arms fall onto my shoulders. He breaks into a sob.

"Hey, hey there."

"Sorry."

"Don't be sorry."

"It's just that you're such a kind and understanding man."

"What's so kind and understanding about pissing on a man who wants it?"

He breaks into a huge laugh of relief.

"You're still my buddy."

His breathing returns to normal. He gets down on his knees and in a single swoop swallows me whole. I'm speechless at his lack of gag reflex. He pulls my hands to the back of his head. I know what he wants, and I oblige.

I begin thrusting into his sweet mouth slowly at first. I'm even more impressed that he hasn't choked on my cock, so I increase my tempo. I turn into a piston, imagining his mouth to be the same as his beautiful asshole. He grunts and groans. His throat muscles are like silk. No resistance whatsoever. "Aw, fuck," I moan.

I look down on him. He's taken his sticky cock out of its pouch and stroking it.

The sight of him getting hard a second time so soon after shooting pushes me over the edge. I don't even say a word as I suddenly stop thrusting and hold his head still. I spurt seven times down his throat. It feels as if my entire insides have come out of that piss hole of mine and yet come back inside me to make me whole again.

I start to feel a bit woozy in my head; almost a headache.

I feel almost unable to breathe, but Jack stands up and simply radiates as he forcibly swallows the rest of my cum.

I look down at his thick stub of erection and smile.

"What?"

"Fuck me," I say. "Jack, I want you to."

He inhales.

I bend down and spit copiously all over his piss-dripping cock, lathering all over it with my sweaty palms, and spread the spit with my tongue. I hold up my hand and he spits even more onto my palm. Our spit mixed all over his cock to my satisfaction, I stand up and anchor my hands against the wall.

The sensation of his unusually long tongue makes me gasp involuntarily. I've had fingers and toys and cocks up my ass, but never a tongue that long touching places where no tongue had never been. Even though I know I don't have any cum left in my balls, I stroke myself to a semi-hardon.

He works my hole hard with his tongue.

"Enough already," I beg. "Just fuck your Daddy."

He snorts. "No, I wanna be your Daddy. You be my boy."

I twist and grab his face. "I'm anything you want me to be. Just fuck me and *own* me."

I return to facing the wall and feel the brunt of his cock weasel in. I crouch down a bit lower to accommodate his height, and he slides right in.

I gasp. He is *thick*. As he pushes himself further in, the tip of his short cock nabs my prostate gland. Bull's eye.

"Fuck!" I nearly scream. I don't understand why so many men are size queens when shorter cocks can really nail that hot spot much better. "Fuck!"

I feel his bruised hands grip my hipbones as he positions himself.

"Boy, do you want Daddy to fuck you?"

I whimper. "Fuck yes."

"I didn't hear you." He is already grinding in and out of me, slow and sure, as his hands turn into a vise grip on my hips.

"Daddy, please fuck me." I am rarely in the position of having to beg, so this feels new to me. "Please!"

He moves and angles himself slowly, as if the head of his cock is probing the rest of my nether regions.

"Daddy, please."

"Shut up, boy. I'll fuck you, and when I fuck you, you won't be able to walk for weeks!"

Somehow being treated like that turns me on. I'm no longer touching myself. I look down. I'm leaking precum like crazy.

"Dad?"

"What, boy?"

"Just ram it in. Hard!"

"Like this?" I am unprepared for the sweet jolt of pain and pleasure as he assaults fury and love against my defenseless joy button.

His absolute command of my helpless body takes my breath away. I have no words, not even a moan, as he pounds my ass so fast that I feel machine-gunned. The elevator lurches from our thrusts.

My cock has never been harder. It needs to fuck. And badly.

His wild thrusts bob my cock up against my belly, so much that I feel lightly slapped. My belly is splattered with precum.

"Boy, are you my boy?"

I finally find my voice. "Yes."

"Good! 'Cause here it co*mmmmes*."

I try not to lose my balance from the wall as I feel the force of his sperm volleying deep inside me. I lose my breath, all language.

He grunts and then laughs lightly. He wraps his arms around me and kisses my sweaty back. "You were fucking fantastic! I'd have never pegged you as a boy."

"I wasn't until just now."

He sighs and pulls slowly out of me. I turn.

His eyes rocket down to my straining erection and he grins. "My turn."

"What?"

Jack positions himself against the wall. "Daddy wants you to fuck him."

And so I do. We share spit and wrap it all over my cock. He doesn't dare touch my nipples — he knows that I'm too close to the edge.

Pulling aside his ass straps, I guide myself into him. His hole is like butter. I stand still for a moment inside him. His ass muscles are opening and squeezing the entire length of my cock like a fist. The feeling of his inner heat is just sublime. "Oh, man."

"Wow," he says.

"What?"

"Your dick's *really* throbbing."

"It better be, or I'd be dead by now!"

He chuckles but I stop him as I give him three unexpectedly fast thrusts, rocking the elevator. I shoot and shoot and shoot inside him.

Done, I wrap my arms around that sweaty and panting belly of his, not wanting to let myself out of his talented ass and not wanting to stop kissing the sides of his neck, his ears, his beard. I spit all over his hairy back and lick up my saliva.

With a deep sigh, he finally breaks the spell. "Well, this place stinks. But in a good way."

We laugh as I pull my withered self out of him.

As he puts his clothes back on, I watch.

"Hey. Go put your clothes on," Jack says. "Boy." He grins.

I don't know why hearing that makes me feel warm inside; hell, I have two kids of my own! There are definitely some things that my wife could never understand, and this is one of them. I pick my clothes off the floor and put them on.

As he unlocks the WAIT button in the elevator, he smiles.

"What?"

"I said you'd be sucking my cock by the end of day, didn't I?"

"That you did." I pull him into my arms and kiss him smack on the lips.

The doors suddenly slide open to find Ernie looking rather incensed. "Finally!"

"What?"

"I got stuff in my car, you know." He sniffs. "Did you two … ?"

We both try not to giggle.

Ernie reaches over to press the GARAGE button.

"Hey," I say. "Look at me."

Ernie turns. "What?"

"You know that guy you dumped?"

"What about him?"

"He's a very, *very* sweet guy. Everybody knows you're an asshole □"

Jack slaps my arm hard. "Don't talk that way to my clients."

"Here, the bear community's small. We all need to learn how to forgive one another. Maybe you should ask for his forgiveness. Just ... be nice to everybody, you know?"

He looks away. We hear him holding his breath until the elevator doors open at last. He trots quickly to his car. He never looks back at us. Not even once.

Jack grabs my hand and kisses it. "Come on, my boy. Time to go home."

Smith Kendall*'s story, "Duplex/Complex," is his first publication. He lives in a very small town on the edge of Nebraska.*

"Waafrneeaasuu!!"

Jerry L. Wheeler

"Ooohhh, yeah! That's it, *papi!* Fuck me harder! *Harder!* Fuck my *mangina!!!*"

Harvey's dick wilted faster than microwaved lettuce.

He pulled out of Eduardo's ass, concentrating on getting his erection back so he could at least come. It only half worked, but at last he coaxed out a gooey stream that shot halfway up to Eduardo's chin. Panting, Harvey flopped forward on the bed, landing beside Eduardo, who grabbed a warm, wet towel from the bedside table and mopped his smooth chest.

"Mmm, nice," Eduardo said as he snaked one muscled arm around Harvey's back. Harvey turned over and stared up at the ceiling, tracing a crack in the plaster until Eduardo started snoring softly and snuggled into his armpit.

Dammit, Harvey thought. *This is a great guy — he's a good kisser, he's really nice and he's not an alcoholic like the last two. He even has a job, for Chrissakes, and that's better than the last four. He's handsome, he's smart and he makes me feel good about myself. And then there are those eyes – warm, brown and eager. They turn me into a puddle every time I look into them. If it's not love, it's the closest I've been in a long time. It's the mangina thing that kills it.*

Okay, he could be a little hairier, too, but … mangina?

Harvey had been able to ignore it the first time. Caught up in the passion of the moment, the word had rolled right out of his ears when Eduardo screamed it. It barely registered. The second and third times, he heard it but it didn't matter. Somewhere around the fifth or sixth time, though, it became irritating. Now, hearing it was like rubbing his dick on a cheese grater.

Eduardo was a gentle soul, easily hurt. Harvey knew that from the second date, when he'd happened to mention in passing that the *paella* Eduardo made for dinner was a touch too spicy for his ulcer. Harvey had to eat three helpings to quell his tears. No, a direct confrontation was definitely out of the question.

He looked down at Eduardo as he slept, his steady, rhythmic breaths tickling the small hairs on his side, and he smiled. *How could I be so petty?* he wondered. *It's only a word, right?* He closed his eyes and tried to sleep, but the word seemed to be imprinted on his eyelids in flowing, femmy script.

Mangina.

His balls recoiled, drawing up into his body as if he'd just been plunged into a cold swimming pool. He didn't know what he was going to do, but he'd have to do something. Soon.

He managed to avoid sex the next morning by letting Eduardo sleep late, then rushing him to get ready for the day ahead, but Eduardo was staying the weekend, so he wasn't going to be able to put him off that night. Once they got home and took a nap, Eduardo's *mangina* would be primed and ready to go. As it was, Harvey barely held him off through breakfast.

"It's a long drive to the Renaissance Faire," Harvey told him through a long, hard kiss at the front door.

Eduardo reached down and squeezed Harvey's hard dick. "Let's stay here for a while, and you drive me."

Harvey finally got them on the road, reaching the *faux* castle gates as trumpets blared and the King and Queen began the morning processional. Eduardo waved away the busty wenches who greeted every entrant to the realm with a sloppy, smeary kiss.

"No girls," he insisted, turning to Harvey and giving him a full-on kiss with tongue as several nearby mothers shielded their children's eyes from the depravity while their husbands looked on with shock and disbelief that this was happening at a family venue.

Harvey chuckled and hugged him as they kissed. He loved Eduardo's fierce insistence on being who he was, and Eduardo was big enough to intimidate anyone who dared question him. He was about six two, with well-defined arms, massive legs and a solid, gym-built chest. He had a bit of a gut, but Harvey found that hot.

They walked around the Faire, enjoying turkey legs and cold beer, stopping to watch sword-swallowers, jugglers, and magicians. Eduardo especially liked the falconer's show, never taking his eyes off the birds. "They are so beautiful," he whispered to Harvey. He bought Harvey a set of Pan's pipes, and Harvey bought him a short, black leather vest with two crossed swords stitched in white on the back.

"Thank you, *papi*," he said, stripping off his A-shirt on the spot and donning it. The sight of that bronze body in the short vest got Harvey hard instantly. The lady who ran the stand murmured an appreciative comment that turned to a mild curse of disappointment when Eduardo took Harvey in his arms for a long, wet, thank-you kiss. Had it not been for their little problem, Harvey would have put an Out of Order sign on the nearest privy and fucked him senseless then and there.

Taking a break from shopping, they sat down on a sun-dappled log and sipped their beers. Eduardo unfolded the map of the grounds.

"What do you want to do next?" he asked.

Harvey looked around to get his bearings, and that's when he saw it right in front of them. It was just another fortune-teller's tent — the placard outside said Gypsy Davey — but under Palmistry, Tarot Reading, and Crystal Tunings was a menu item that caught his eye.

Magick words a specialty!

Harvey couldn't believe what he was thinking, but the thought wouldn't leave him alone. Not that he believed in crap like that. All his life he'd been a confirmed skeptic about all things mystical, but this mangina problem called for creative solutions. And he was desperate. Eduardo must have seen him looking at the tent.

"You go in for that stuff?" Eduardo asked, pointing toward Gypsy Davey's.

Harvey smiled, challenging him playfully. "And what if I did?"

Eduardo chuckled. "It's your money," he replied. "Go ahead — do it if you want. I'll look at the map while you get your fortune told. And when they tell you, 'You are going to meet a tall, dark, handsome stranger,' tell them you already have a boyfriend." He laughed and sipped his beer.

"I'll be right back."

Surprised he was actually going through with it, Harvey stood up, walked across the trail to the tent, pushed aside the flap and entered. The place smelled like feet, sweaty silk, and Egg McMuffin.

"Sorry, dude — haven't finished breakfast yet," explained the young man sitting barefoot behind a low makeshift counter that held a Mickey D's bag. He wore a purple scarf wrapped around his head, harem pants, and a brocade vest with no shirt, revealing a mat of dark hair on his chest. Harvey saw muffin crumbs sticking to the wax of his handlebar moustache.

"You look kinda young for this," Harvey said.

"Do you think the Fates speak only to old crones?" His accent was lousy. "What do you seek?"

"A magic word." He felt like a moron saying it out loud.

"For what purpose? To charm a young lady? To make an enemy feel your power? To make money, perhaps?"

Harvey lifted the tent flap. "See that guy sitting on the log over there?"

Gypsy Davey nodded.

"He's my boyfriend, and I want to butch him up some."

"He looks pretty butch already."

"Okay, maybe not butch — how about ... more *bearish*?" That would have to do. He wasn't about to explain the whole *mangina* thing to a fake gypsy who couldn't even do a decent Slavic accent.

Gypsy Davey fiddled with the end of his moustache. "Ah yes," he said after a few moments. "I believe I have what you need. It is a word of transformation – very ancient and quite potent, indeed. It must be spoken in the throes of passion only. The word is: *waafrneeaasuu*."

"Um — could you write that down?"

"Writing down a magick word robs it of its powers. Ten dollars, please."

Harvey pulled out his wallet and handed the ten over. "Okay, if you can't write it down, could you at least *say* it again? Or will that cost me another ten bucks?"

"Waafrneeaasuu."

"Waafrneeaasuu," Harvey repeated. "Got it. What if I just walk up to him and say it now?"

Gypsy Davey rolled his eyes. "You're the kind of guy they put directions on shampoo bottles for, aren't you? Just whisper it in his ear the next time you make love, and all shall be as you wish."

"Right. Thanks."

"Whatta *schmuck,*" he heard Gypsy Davey mutter as the tent flap dropped behind him.

Gentle kisses tickled the back of Harvey's neck, waking him up from his nap. He thought about jamming his face further into the pillow and waving Eduardo away. No, that would cause more problems than it would solve. I can't do that to him, he thought. He didn't want to deal with the situation, but there was no way out of it. Maybe Eduardo wouldn't say it this time.

The sheets scratched Harvey's sunburned legs as he rolled over, drew Eduardo close and kissed him. He tasted like the mead they'd had at the fair, sweet and addictive, and Harvey's dick hardened as he ran his hands over Eduardo's smooth, hard back muscles. Eduardo's fingertips traced Harvey's nipples and skated down the hair of his chest to his cock. Eduardo broke the kiss, his tongue trailing across Harvey's neck.

"Mmm, nice," Eduardo breathed in his ear, gripping his dick. "Such a hard *pinga* — you should have let me take care of that this morning."

Harvey felt Eduardo's cock stiffening against the outside of his thigh and knew he'd be getting his *pinga* sucked in a few seconds. That's key, he thought. If I can just keep something in his mouth at all times, I've got it made. True to form, Eduardo slid down the sheets and began to work Harvey's balls with his tongue.

The silence was heaven, and so was Eduardo's warm mouth on his cock. Harvey was hornier than he thought, and he began to buck against Eduardo's head, fucking his mouth until he started to feel a load building up. He grabbed his head and pulled Eduardo up for a long kiss as he rolled over onto him and got into position.

"Yesss," Eduardo hissed. "*Papi* wants my *mmman—*" Harvey sealed his mouth tight with a vacuum kiss, as if he could suck the word right out of Eduardo's brain, but Eduardo managed a smothered moan. Harvey knew it was a lost cause. He'd get that word out somehow. Harvey felt his dick start to shrink, but then he remembered Gypsy Davey's ten-dollar word. Feeling desperate and ridiculous at the same time, Harvey unsealed Eduardo's mouth and whispered in his ear.

"*Waafrneeaasuu …*"

Nothing.

Maybe I said it wrong, Harvey thought, but he felt too stupid to say it again. *There's ten bucks shot to shit.*

Eduardo's moaning continued unabated, though its timbre suddenly changed; it became lower and more gruff than before. And Harvey had the weird sensation of grass growing beneath him, like the time-lapse photography in a lawn fertilizer commercial. He looked down and saw a covering of hair on Eduardo's chest where there had been none — lengthening and darkening before his eyes.

"What th—" Harvey looked into Eduardo's warm, curious eyes for an answer. They were still as warm and curious as ever, but they were now set into a face unlike the one Harvey had laid down for a nap with. This one was covered with hair and had a snout instead of a mouth, its breath reeking of something Harvey couldn't identify but sure as hell wasn't mead.

"Mrrrppphhh!!" Eduardo growled into Harvey's ear.

Eduardo's strong arms, now shaggy with hair, closed around Harvey's back. He heard the clack of claws and felt their sharp hardness pressing into his skin, but that wasn't all. Eduardo's erection was pressing into his thigh too — only now it was considerably larger than before. Harvey didn't have time to look, however. Before he realized what was happening, Eduardo shifted his weight to the right, neatly flipped Harvey over and, well … *bearbacked* him.

Harvey and Eduardo were back at the fair before the morning trumpets blew, waiting in line for the gates to open. People stared and pointed at Eduardo, but he didn't seem to mind. He sat patiently leashed at Harvey's side, scratching every now and then at the studded collar around his hairy neck, smartly outfitted in tan cargo shorts and the leather vest Harvey had bought for him the day before.

Gypsy Davey sat outside his tent eating an apple. "Good lookin' bear," he said as they approached.

"That's not a bear, it's my boyfriend."

"Mrrrppphhh," Eduardo added.

"I thought I recognized the vest." He threw the apple core over the fence behind the tent and held the flap open for them. "C'mon in." He sat down behind the low counter and crossed his legs in a tight lotus position. "So, what is it you seek today?"

"*What is it* ..." Harvey's temper rose, but he tried to control himself. Flying off the handle wasn't going to get Eduardo changed back. "Ummm, let me see," he said, "how about something to kinda tone down your magic word — maybe an adjective or an adverb or something."

"Does this look like grammar class? You wanted a bear, you got a bear. And you're not gettin' your ten bucks back, either. Gypsy profit margin sucks this season." The accent was gone.

"I don't give a *shit* about your profit margin," Harvey said through clenched teeth. "Have you ever been cornholed by a fuckin' *bear*? It ain't pretty — I mean, I'm versatile, but Jesus *Christ* ... You gotta change him back."

"No can do."

"Whaddya mean by that?"

"Mrrrppphh?" Eduardo looked confused, his eyes meeting Harvey's.

"Well — once done, magic's kinda tough to undo."

"Yeah?" Harvey slid his hand down the leash to Eduardo's collar and put his finger on the release button. "Well, you better *find* a way, or there's gonna be one pissed off bear loose in your tent."

Eduardo shifted his eyes to Gypsy Davey and began to rumble, flexing his clawed paws. "*Mrrrppphh!!*"

"Okay, *okay*," the gypsy said. Harvey could have sworn he saw his harem pants turn brown as he grabbed a cell phone and started dialing. "Hang on a minute."

"Who are you calling?"

"My grandmother in Craiova."

"Craiova? Where the hell's *that*?"

"Romania — just keep the fuckin' bear cool, all right?"

Harvey took his hand away from Eduardo's collar and started petting him. "Sssshhh, it's gonna be okay."

"*Bunica*?" he said, "*Buna dimeneata, bunica — ca s'schimbare s'urs*?"

Harvey tuned out the conversation since he couldn't understand it anyway. Eduardo never took his eyes off the gypsy, but at least he stopped growling.

Then Gypsy Davey turned pale. "*Voi sigur*?" he said. "*Multumesc, bunica. La revedere*." He flipped the cell phone shut.

"What'd she say?"

"You're not gonna like this, dude."

"What?"

"She said the bear will tell you what to say."

"The *bear*? What the fuck is *that* supposed to mean?"

"Look, man — she's a hundred and two years old. She's forgotten more about magic words and gypsy curses than I'll ever know. If she says the bear will tell you what to say, the bear will tell you what to say. Trust me."

"Like we have a choice," Harvey snorted. "C'mon, Eduardo."

Eduardo sniffed and scratched his armpit with his hind leg. "Mmrrp-phh," he said, following Harvey out of the tent.

"Losers," Gypsy Davey muttered, putting up his OUT TO LUNCH sign.

Sloppy bear-licks coated the back of Harvey's neck, waking him up from his nap. He tried to bury his face in his spit-soaked pillow, but it was like burrowing into a sponge. He waved the bear away, but Eduardo was insistent. Harvey felt his hairy warmth beside him and heard his claws ripping through the comforter. And the mattress. And the box springs.

"Not now, Eduardo," he said, wrinkling his nose at the feral stench that filled the bedroom. He was getting used to it, though. There was something *primeval* about it — elemental and savage. Musky but spicy at the same time; a piquant odor that had an undeniable, animalistic urge to it. In fact, as unbelievable as it was, the smell was making him horny.

Harvey snuggled his back into Eduardo's underside, feeling the bear's belly hairs tickling his back and ass. His dick started rising. Harvey was a little uneasy about this at first, but then he started thinking about it. It's not like this is a *strange* bear, he said to himself. It's not a one-night stand — it's

Eduardo. As if to reassure himself of that, he turned over and looked the bear square in the eyes.

And he saw what he'd seen the first time they met. Warm, soft brown eyes, curious and eager to please. Eager to love. Eyes that had always been able to melt his heart, and this was no exception. He reached his arms around the bear and squeezed him as hard as he could. He would have kissed him if he could have figured out how, but he settled for kissing the end of his big, black nose.

"Mmmrrppphh," Eduardo bear-sighed in response. Apparently, he'd noticed Harvey's erection too. One hairy paw came up between Harvey's legs, tickling his balls softly with his claws as the rough pads scraped the shaft of Harvey's dick with delicious friction. Harvey ground his cock harder into Eduardo's paw as the bear began licking Harvey's neck. Harvey knew that, on some level, other people might find this whole thing strange, but he couldn't help what was happening. Eduardo's tongue felt smooth and slick as it slobbered a wide swath of pleasure down his chest. Harvey's dick was at full mast as he anticipated what it would feel like on his cock and balls. A bear blow-job. Harvey couldn't help but smile as he tugged on Eduardo's ear to get his attention.

"Watch the teeth," he said with a grin. He could have sworn Eduardo grinned back.

Harvey felt like a postage stamp as Eduardo's tongue ran over every crevice of his crotch then worked its way underneath for the rim job. His ecstasy was only slightly hampered by the thought of Eduardo's huge bear-cock, which was plainly on the rise. It had hurt like hell last night, but he hadn't really been prepared. He wasn't sure he was prepared now, but Eduardo had turned into a total top.

Among other things, he said to himself with a chuckle.

Eduardo centered himself between Harvey's legs, threw his ankles into the air and leaned forward. "Mmrrrppphhh," he growled.

"Mmrrrpphhh," Harvey responded, trying to match Eduardo's breathy grumble.

Eduardo suddenly got a little smaller.

Something clicked in Harvey's brain. *The bear will tell you what to say.*

"Mmrrppphhh," Harvey said again.

Eduardo's claws began retracting and his fur started getting shorter.

"Mrrrppphhh!! Mrrrppphhh!! Mmrrrppphhh!"

Eduardo's snout flattened out and his breath returned to normal. Harvey kept repeating it until Eduardo was at last back to himself, except for a thick coating of fur on his chest and legs.

"*Papi* ..." he said, but Harvey didn't give him a chance to say anything else. He turned him over and fucked him hard, gluing their mouths together with so much lust, love and relief they could barely grunt and gasp for air. Harvey pumped away frantically as Eduardo groaned and squirmed beneath him until finally they both shot in geysers of cum, Eduardo not even touching his own cock.

Harvey collapsed beside Eduardo, soaked with sweat, cum, and bear-spit. The bed was a tangled, sticky puddle of ripped sheets and blankets that clutched at Harvey's skin as he put his arm over Eduardo's now hairy chest.

Eduardo settled into his usual position beneath Harvey's armpit. "*Mmmannngiiiinnnaaah!*" he said.

Harvey sighed, then smiled.

He was just going to have to get used to it.

Former staff writer for Out Front Colorado, one of America's oldest and largest GLBT publications, ***Jerry L. Wheeler*** *has appeared in many anthologies, including* Law of Desire: Tales of Gay Male Lust and Obsession, I Do! *and* I Like It Like That: True Tales of Gay Desire *as well as online in* Velvet Mafia *and Greg Wharton's terrifically queer* Inverte *blog. Be sure to catch his book reviews on* Out in Print *at <www.outinprint.net>.*

Old Majestic

Tim Morrison

After a very tense week at work, I packed an overnight bag and hit the highway after Friday morning rush hour. I intended to drive up 101 as far as I felt like driving and stay the weekend somewhere. Didn't matter where I ended up as long as I could find a comfortable motel or motor lodge and a decent restaurant where I could get meals. I brought no cell phone, no laptop, nothing but clothes, personal necessities, and a book. I didn't even care whether the motel had cable, much less a television.

It was a typical Northern California February: a light rain fell started to fall, and the sound of the windshield wipers was almost soothing. Traffic wasn't too bad, and once I got away from the city, I felt my mind ease off the events of the past week. I went on autopilot, surfing radio stations for good music, thoughts drifting in and out of my mind. I felt relaxed. This was my own adventure, and I'd make it up as I went along.

Hours later I found myself in Humboldt County, and I figured I'd drive a bit further and call it a day. After filling up the car and taking a leak, I needed food. As I sat in a diner across from the gas station, munching a BLT, I paged through a travel guide I'd picked up at the diner entrance and saw an ad for a motel to check out. I finished my meal and approached the cash register to pay when I dropped my wallet, overstuffed with receipts, membership cards, and ID. I scrambled to pick up the bits of paper and plastic and noticed a business card:

ROY PETERS

IDLEWOOD FURNITURE & WOODWORK

There was an address, along with a phone number and the words *In Beautiful Humboldt County.*

"Excuse me, ma'am?" I asked the waitress at the register. "Can you tell me if this is nearby?" She took the card and peered at it over the eyeglasses perched on her nose. "Oh, sure! That's only about 15 minutes from here, 20 tops. Need directions?"

"Please. That would be great," I smiled.

Hastily scribbled directions in hand, I got back into my car and thought to myself, *This trip could possibly get more interesting.*

I met Roy Peters just over a year ago at a Sunday beer bust. I hadn't planned to go anywhere that day, but I got bored and instead headed over, paid my seven bucks and perched myself near the pool table. It was still early, and the place couldn't even be considered a fifth full. I figured I'd leave once it started to get too busy. I saw a tall figure come through the door but couldn't get a good look with all the outdoor light surrounding him. When the doors closed, I noticed he was much too well-dressed for the place: suit, tie, the whole works. I would consider myself a regular at this place, but I'd never seen him before. I saw that we probably matched each other in height, but he had an edge on me in the bulk department. The suit fit him well, his blond hair and beard were neatly cut, and I imagined he probably was visiting from out of town on business. I don't get the whole suit fetish thing, but he was so damned handsome in his that I might have reconsidered.

The space beside me was free; he smiled in my direction and strode toward me. He nodded and said, "Howdy." I tipped my cup to him in mid-sip. "Afternoon, yourself," I said. Then I clammed up. I'm really not the outgoing sort and rarely make the first move. This is why I usually went home alone.

"Seems a little empty today," he said.

Good. He broke the ice. Once I'm past that, I'm OK. "Nah, it's early yet. Won't get busy for another hour or so. But if I were you, I'd get out before then."

He looked at me amusingly. "Oh, yeah? How do you figure?"

"You look too good for this place. Some drunk is liable to spill beer on you and ruin your clothes when you have to squeeze your way out of here."

"Ah, I thought this was your way of giving a brush-off."

"Not hardly. I'm Terry," I said, extending my hand.

"I'm Roy." His hand was rough and strong. I wished he was in the usual bar drag so I could get a better idea of his body and what it looked like.

He explained that he was on his way to a wedding reception for a cousin at one of the country clubs south of the city. He had time to kill, so he decided to stop in for a drink. This was the first time in years that he set foot in the place. I mentally cursed the cousin for having her wedding on this day. I mean, here I was, with a hot man in a bar where I usually blend into the walls, and he was only going to be there for a brief time. His friendliness was a refreshing break from all the typical bar cruising that amounted to little, if anything.

I learned he was 47, a native Californian, and a woodworker up north. I told him my brief story: I came to the city eight years ago at age 37 and was ready to leave about four years into my time here. "Yeah, the city's not for everyone. Very transitory," he said, shaking his head. He glanced at the wall clock. "Thanks for the chat, but I really have to get going. Let me give you my card." He fished around in a jacket pocket and handed it to me. "Give me a shout sometime and maybe we can meet for a drink next time I'm down here."

"Hey, have a good time," I said. He winked and rushed out the door.

I looked at the card he gave me. It was his business card with an address and phone number, no e-mail address or website. I stuffed it into my wallet and thought to myself that I'd wait a respectable few weeks and then give him a call. The following weekend — so sue me — I picked up the phone and dialed his number. No answering machine picked up after a dozen rings, so I hung up. After a couple more fruitless attempts, the card went back into my wallet and forgotten.

Thanks to the waitress's directions, I easily found Roy's shop. A car and a truck were parked out in front, and I sort of hoped that he was busy with customers in case I chickened out. A bell above the door rang as I stepped into a modest showroom packed with various pieces of woodwork. Roy was talking to a man about a china hutch while the man's wife idly looked at the pieces in the showroom.

I know next to nothing about woodwork, but his work looked of excellent quality to me. I traced the curlicues on a highboy and wished I had an apartment big enough to keep it. It was made of cherry (according to the price tag tied around the door handle) and cost about a month's salary for me. I was so lost in looking at the detail work that I hadn't noticed the couple leave the shop.

"Can I help you?" Roy said behind me.

I turned away from the highboy to face him. "Is there something in particular you're interested in?" he asked.

"Uh … just driving by and thought I'd take a look," I said. *Great,* I thought to myself. *He doesn't recognize me.*

"Look all you want. Let me know if you have any questions about anything."

He went behind the counter and started to read a newspaper. I took a glimpse of him. He had shaved off his beard but looked to be in the process of growing it back, his face covered in heavy, blond-and-white stubble. The sleeve of his blue work shirt strained around his upper arm covered in thick, honey-blond fur.

I found several small, wooden boxes, each about the size of a child's shoebox. Grooves were carved into all six sides and at the front was a drawer with a bear-shaped handle. I thought it would look good on my dresser. Or maybe … hey, it would be great to use as a condom stash! The price was right, too: $20.

He looked up from his paper when I approached. "One of my best-selling items!" he said. I just sort of smiled and said nothing. "This is going to sound weird, but … have we met? You look awfully familiar."

"Didn't you have a cousin who got married about a year ago?" I asked.

He paused and then his eyes widened. "Oh, yeah!" he said. "Your name is — don't tell me, I'll get it — Terry! Right? Your name is Terry."

I nodded and smiled. "Yep, you got it."

"Hey, good to see you!" He clapped a hand on my shoulder. "What brings you up this way?"

I told him about my escape plans. "Hard to believe you've lived this long in the state and haven't gotten any further than Marin," he shook his head. "I love it up here. Hey, wanna look around out back? There are some redwoods a short walk away from here. Let me just put on something warmer first."

He ducked into the back of the shop where I caught a glimpse of him pulling a thermal shirt over his broad back. He grabbed a jacket from a hook.

We left the shop and we set out on a path at the rear of the shop. I flipped up the hood of my jacket and walked beside Roy. I breathed in the scent of the trees the surrounded us. The gentle rain had not stopped, and I didn't care. I didn't find it dreary in the least; it just seemed fitting, and I liked the sound of the raindrops on my hood.

"You know, I had hoped to hear from you, but I just figured you weren't interested," he said. "I was smacking myself in the head later for not asking for your number."

"I did try to call a couple times." I dug the card out of my pocket and handed it to him. He looked at it and said, "Man, I am more of an idiot than I thought! I gave you a card with my old number on it! I thought I'd thrown all of those away!"

"No worries," I said. "I'm here, right? Though I have to admit I wouldn't be here had I not spilled my wallet all over the place and noticed I still had your card."

"Well, I'm glad you did," he grinned. "And right over here is something I want to show you." He bounded ahead of me, leaving the path. I caught up to find him peering up at a huge, old redwood. We were surrounded by them; I didn't know what was so special about this one. He pulled me around to the other side. "I call him Old Majestic. I reckon he's close to 200 feet, but I have no idea how old he is. C'mon inside. I hope you're not claustrophobic."

Roy stood inside the hollow of the tree and moved to make room for me. I had to stoop over a bit to keep from bumping the top of my head. "Sometimes I like to come out here to think," he said. "It's very peaceful in here." It struck me how quiet it was inside. I couldn't hear the rain through the thick, insulating interior of the tree. I reached to touch the wood and was surprised to find that it felt smooth as if it had been polished. We watched the intensifying rain from the safety and embrace of the old tree, close, almost touching each other. We didn't speak; speaking didn't seem right.

I looked at Roy to see him smiling at me. He reached around my waist and pulled me closer to him. I slipped a hand into his back pocket and gave his ass a gentle squeeze. Our lips found each other in a single kiss imbued with intention. When his tongue slipped into my mouth, a rush of blood raced to my groin, and I pulled him to me with a firm grip on his ass. He was already hard, his warm mound pressed against mine. His hands found my nipples, and he gave them a firm pinch in his work-roughened hands. If it was possible, my cock hardened even more; it needed to be free or else it would split wide open. I explored his belly and chest with my hands, and the thick hair under his clothes felt like burlap under cotton. I wanted to be under the weight of his body, but I knew I wouldn't last the trek back up to his place. We would finish each other here, inside Old Majestic.

I backed away from him and pulled his shirt out from under the waistband of his jeans. We laughed as we both struggled to free him from the shirt, settling for stretching its hem behind his neck but otherwise leaving it on. I buried my face in all that chest fur, wet with his sweat, and latched onto a meaty tit.

"Ohhhh, fucker … that's just what I like," he groaned. I wanted to rip off the rest of his clothes, but I was going to make this gift last, revealing it bit by bit. He brought my face to his and kissed me deeply, his tongue nearly reaching my throat. He fingered the hard stubs beneath my shirt, his calloused fingers sensitizing me. I yanked open his belt and undid his pants. He was wearing flannel boxers with a sticky wet spot across the front. He helped me extract his hard, thick cock, and I grabbed it in my paw. I could not get my fingers all the way around it. He was uncut — an extra treat — and I swiped a finger into his foreskin, all around his glans. I knew he'd be sensitive there, and his body shook as he held onto my shoulders with both hands.

I dropped to my knees and buried my face in his crotch, rubbing his cock all over my face, anointing myself with his precum, licking his heavy balls. I rooted my nose in the rough patch of fur at the base of his cock. Man, it was the finest smell outside a bottle of cologne. I could tell he showered with pine tar soap that morning, and his own essence complemented it. I could have spent the rest of the day sniffing around him, all over him. He smelled of the forest.

He guided his cock to my mouth, and I eagerly opened to accept him, his hands firmly holding my head in place as he fucked my face. I gagged on him a little, and he released some of the pressure on my head and let me work on him. He had the best kind of cock there is for sucking or fucking:

narrow at the head and wider at the base. He moaned and gasped at the feeling of my tongue inside his foreskin as I slurped around it. Now that I'd gotten used to the girth of his dick, he began to fuck my face again. I met him thrust for thrust, and the noises he made were getting more urgent. He was as close as could be, the head of his cock swelling at the back of my throat.

And then he pulled out of my mouth completely. I gasped for breath as he pulled me up from my knees. I held his cock to keep it warm from the coolness of the air outside, and he kissed me gently. "You're gonna come first, buddy," he said. And with that he backed me into the wall of the tree. My pants were pulled open and down my shaking legs, and he took me in his mouth all the way to my balls in one stroke. His spit dripped down my fuzzy balls and down my thighs, his tight, sucking mouth clamped onto me, up and down, up and down. The sensations were so intense that I had to leave my body ever so slightly — focus on something else — or else I'd pass out. I watched the muscles of his back flex as he worked on me and felt myself retreat.

He pulled off my cock with a slurp and breathed heavy. "Need a rest, bud?" he gasped. I squeezed the back of his neck in assent. He nursed and licked the end of my cock softly, not wanting to break total contact with it, and then he positioned himself to do serious work on it. He took me with less urgency at first and built up to a rhythm. I began to peak; I could feel my balls crawling up into my groin and would soon deliver what he wanted from me. I peaked, and peaked, and peaked and then ... nothing.

"Listen," I breathed. "I've never been able to come from getting sucked off, much less standing up. Feels great, what you're doing, but ..."

"Ah, bullshit. I'll make you come. Let ol' Roy take care of you." With that, he stuck two of his fingers in his mouth, wetting them heavily with his spit, and he worked them between my legs, under my balls, to my asshole. He shoved his wet fingers into my tight hole, all the way to his knuckles. It hurt, but in the most pleasurable way.

My knees bent slightly to give him better access, and even with my back against the inner wall of the tree for support, I felt as if my full weight was supported with just his forearm. He sucked me back into his mouth, down to my balls again, the heel of his hand on my taint, his fingers deep in my ass. My prostate was clamped into this vice grip, the suction of his mouth intensified, his hand worked on me, and I felt my legs shudder and warm with heat. "Awww ... *Gawd!*" I shouted and my balls tightened into a knot. He gave one last squeeze, and my jism boiled out of me, like fire jetting out of me into his tight, sucking mouth. I could have sworn I felt my feet leave the ground briefly, impaled as I was on his hand. I could feel every spurt coming out of me against his tongue. He moaned around my cock, and I saw that he was working on himself, his other hand rapidly jacking himself off. Unmistakably he was caught up in his own orgasm. He stopped sucking and swallowed my load down his throat. I pulled myself out of him, and he licked the last drops oozing out of me. The darkness in the tree kept me from seeing the white drops of his come on the floor.

The air inside Old Majestic was moist with our heavy breathing and smelled of sex. Roy hauled himself up and pulled me to him. I tasted my brine on his tongue and reached to squeeze his cock to find it wet and sticky with his own cum.

He chuckled sheepishly. "Sorry, I couldn't wait. But it's OK. I can make more, that's for sure."

We stumbled out of Old Majestic and put ourselves back together. The rain had not stopped. "Do you know where you're headed?" he asked.

I paused and smiled, hoping this was leading to something. "No. Do you have any ideas?"

"Yeah. I think you've found your destination for the weekend." He pulled me to his side and kissed me.

"Yeah," I said. "I think I have."

Tim Morrison*'s work has appeared, under the pseudonym T. S. Wayne in* Bear *and* 100% Beef *magazines, and he contributed to* Bears on Bears: Interviews & Discussions, *by Ron Suresha. He lives with his partner in Minnesota.*

Scruff-Cub

Jeff Mann

Art's waiting for me by his pickup when I arrive. I park my truck beside his and step out. The sun's bright this early October morning, pouring down over southwest Virginia, but the air's chilly, especially up this high, the scenic overlook cresting Draper Mountain. As we'd hoped, there's no one else around. We grin at one another. He tips his cap, I tip mine. We stand side by side for a good minute without speech, looking out over the great drop, over treetops and, far across Draper Valley, the parallel folds of the Blue Ridge. A buzzard glides by, crickets chirp in chorus. Already the sumacs have turned a deep crimson, the tulip trees a pale gold. Far below are the devout Christians, the good country people, the truckers threading I 81, Art's husband and mine. So many people we need to keep unaware.

Well, the secrets get tiresome, but the secrets are worth it. I know that without a doubt, shifting my glance now from Appalachian blue-green hills spotted with autumn's oncoming colors and looking Art full in the face. Such a beautiful boy. He grins again. "Glad you could come, sir. Been a while." Eyes ranging over me, he licks his lips. "Damn, Daddy, you're hot."

What can I do but chuckle? Sleek, young, and smooth seem to be the dominant gay aesthetics these days, and I'm none of those. Art, though, seems to dote on the Daddybear look I've achieved at age 50: bushy graying beard, big arms, and a thick chest that just barely beats out my belly for prominence. And I dote right back. Nothing like a five-foot-eight cub twenty years my junior, a little guy with a scruffy goatee, dense body fur, and a craving for submission to fascinate me to the point of risk-taking and foolishness.

"Sweet hat," Art says, looking up at me and winking. He and I manage to see one another so seldom that we always dress for one another's pleasure when we do meet. After three years of this affair, each man knows well what the other savors. I'm wearing old jeans, a black T-shirt, and black cowboy boots to go with the black straw Shady Brady I picked up last week at the Old Fort Western Store just to give Art a show. I know how much Nashville styles, *Brokeback Mountain*, and cowboys in general heat him up. He, on the other hand, is wearing camo pants, tan work boots, a very tight A-shirt, and a Pulaski Mariners baseball cap. It's the laid-back redneck look I grew up around and find supremely erotic.

"Sweet tank top," I say, "though I'm guessing you're a mite chilly." As is often the case, I'm staring at Art's chest and wishing he were naked. There's always a breeze up here, and its slight chill has, to my pleasure, hardened up his nipples. The little nubs stand up beneath the A-shirt's ribbed cloth, erect and prominent, as if demanding to be seen, as if begging to be fondled. I'm thinking absurdly, metaphorically, of oak buds, sprouting snowdrops, ridge-top signal fires, or cairns. Art's pecs are very full, very hairy, one of the things about him that most besot me. They've always reminded me of tree-covered hills.

"It *is* a little nippy. And I'm guessing you can warm me up," Art says. "Okay, we don't have long. Let's get to this. I'm damned ready for it. Then I'll give you my good news." He heads up the stone steps by the overlook and I follow him into the forest. There's the foundation of a ruined house up here — what a view the inhabitants had, what savage winters they must have weathered — complete with a crumbling fireplace and chimney that conceal us from the road. By the time I've dropped my pants and boxer briefs, Art's pulled off his A-shirt, exposed his own cock, and fallen to his knees. I fill up that handsome goateed mouth, grasping the back of his head and roughly riding his face. He grunts and slobbers, jacking his penis, playing with his own nipples, kneading my ass. Above us, the oaks rustle. Around us, sunlight, slanting through the breeze-restless foliage, dapples the brittle scatter of last year's leaves.

As long as it's been since we've had a chance to touch, as high as our longing for one another has mounted, it takes only a few minutes for me to shoot down Art's throat and him to shoot in his hand. We're dressing when we hear car doors down below in the overlook's parking lot, the piercing cries of children — why do they always have to scream?

"Fuck," I say. "Every time, a goddamned rush." I straighten my hat on my head and spit into the leaves.

"I'll leave first," Art says, tucking in his A-shirt.

Nodding, I wipe a trickle of cum from his goatee. "Looks like you're drooling pearls, Scruff-Cub. Mustn't offend the breeders' delicate sensibilities."

Art snickers, then licks the cum off my fingers. "So, sir, Herb will definitely be attending that overseas conference again. It's the second week in December, the same time you said your honey might be out of town. If I can get some leave days, how about you kidnap me?"

"*Hell*, yes," I reply, giddy at the news. My husbear John is cool with my romps on the side, but Art's partner Herb is incredibly insecure and obsessed with monogamy, so play-time with Art, other than these woodland quickies, is nigh onto impossible. "Is he still checking your cell phone bills and reading your e-mail?"

"Yep," Art sighs. "He's a computer whiz. He's set it up so every message I send is copied to him. As soon as I know the exact dates, I'll snail-mail 'em to you, okay? And please come by the store when you can, please, sir? I love seeing you even if I can't touch you."

With that, he's gone. I linger in the woods for a while so as to avert suspicion. The shrieks of children approach, banishing any peace I might find here. I descend the stone stairs, give the brat-passel and the dumpy parents an ugly look, then head down the mountain in my truck. Sometimes I get so fucking sick of living in a sea of straights.

"The chicken salad's great," John says. We're gobbling take-out sandwiches I've fetched from The Twins Bakery, one of several down-home places we patronize around here. Pulaski's a little mountain town a lot like the one in West Virginia where I grew up, with a decaying economy and ridiculously cheap property values. Four years ago we moved here, after buying a great old Georgian house of solid brick, a hilltop home we would never have been able to afford in more prosperous areas. John telecommutes from home, and I'm a university professor with a short commute but blessed with a schedule more flexible than the usual 9-to-5, so we spend a good bit of time together. He's vanilla; I'm into BDSM. Other than that fairly crucial divergence, we get along very well even after — or perhaps because of — our twelve years together.

"Did you meet Art this morning?" John says, without looking up.

"Yep. He's coming over while you're in Florida, in December. For a week."

"Guess your ropes will get some use. I'm assuming his partner doesn't know this?"

John's always been good at making me feel guilty without even trying. From the beginning, I've been the overly passionate one, the bad boy into rough sex, always restless, often raging, never completely satisfied, racking up tattoos, pointless infatuations, and long shit lists. I'm a Leo. Sometimes it seems like all I am is lion-hunger and lion-anger. John, he's the calm one, the Virgo devoted to order, the one who loves to garden and beautify the house, the one satisfied by quiet evenings at home. He's honesty and integrity embodied. I've been known to lie if it gets me what I want. My lies are smooth and slick, graceful as swans, like most Southerners'.

"No. Herb still doesn't know about us."

"You've got quite the crush on Art, don't you?"

"No," I say. "He's just a fuck. A hot fuck."

John shakes his head and takes another bite of sandwich. I want to say, I wish I were simpler, less crazy and hot-headed, more like you. I want to say, I wish what we had was enough. Nothing's enough for me. I don't know what's wrong with me. I want to say, I'm sorry if my lust and rage hurt you. I want to say, You're so handsome and golden, so full of light. I want to say, Thank you for giving me the freedom to find elsewhere what little I need that you can't provide. Instead I finish my sandwich, put the plates in the dishwasher, and start a load of laundry.

I'm a little in love with Art, I guess. John's right about that, though I keep denying it. Call me greedy. I want a husband *and* a boy. Short, hairy, butch bottoms have always seized my heart in some place dangerously deep. Now if only Art's jealous partner would evaporate, move to Europe, run off with someone else. Ever since I was a kid, I've wanted to smash anything or anyone who gets in my way, who says No to my invariably fervid and often unreasonable desires. This is why I lift weights and pound a punching bag with regularity. It keeps me out of prison.

I'm cogitating these things this November afternoon as I watch Art molding sausage behind the meat counter. He's dressed in his Food City butcher's outfit, a white smock stained with pink. With plastic-gloved hands, he's sculpting a huge vat of sausage into a pig's face. Odd medium, good artist. He's too intent to know I'm watching. By the time he's done, it looks pretty good: long snout, fat cheeks, little folded ears. He adds black-olive eyes for a finishing touch.

"You're the Michelangelo of pork," I say.

Art looks up and smiles. "Howdy, Mr. Jeff," he says. It's thrilling, how pleased he looks to see me. I love his blue eyes, his long slope of a nose, his shaggy head of light brown hair, the way his brown goatee grades into a dusty gold where it frames his mouth. I love his smells of Old Spice and sweat, the way beard stubble so often darkens his face, a scruffy sea joining sideburns and goatee. I love the way he slouches in his ever-present A-shirt, summer evenings after work, smoking on the loading dock back of the store. And, most especially, I love the grunts he makes against a ball gag when my cock slides up his ass.

That's a music I only enjoy once a year, during Herb's conference every December. John, God love him, is either secure enough not to be threatened or knows better than to deny me something I want so badly and get so rarely. He always visits family then, leaving me alone with my boy for that precious week. Don't know how many men would tolerate such a thing, much less my regular rants, resentments, and erratic moods. I guess, meeting him, I lucked out.

"How are the pork and chicken tamales?" I ask Art, pointing to the meat-stuffed cylinders wrapped in cornhusks inside the display case.

He laughs. "Pretty good, sir. As I told you before, they ain't as tasty as the ones I make at home, but they're tolerable."

We're teasing one another, echoing the very first words we exchanged. We met right here, over the Food City meat counter three years ago. Before then, I'd had my eye on his furry face and beefy little physique for months. I'd hang around the meat counter on one pretext or another as often as I could, studying him as he joshed with coworkers, cut and wrapped pork loins and steaks. The first time I saw him out of his butcher's smock, he was leaving the store one July twilight when his shift ended. He was ambling through the parking lot, brown chest hair coursing over the top and out the sides of his A-shirt. He looked up at me, smiled, and lit a cigarette. I smiled back, took in the contrast between that rich dark fur and that ghost-pale garment, took in the chunky pecs and belly making curves of his torso's profile, and was so smitten I almost walked into a stray shopping cart.

Seeing the tamales was the first excuse I could find to strike up a conversation. Running into him at the Roanoke Bear Run that summer's end, realizing he was indeed gay, that was sheer luck, divine intervention. Pretty soon thereafter, our conversations over the meat counter got more interesting, our rendezvous at the Draper Mountain overlook started up. That December was the first time we took advantage of Herb's absence to make Art my week-long captive.

"I want one of those small locally raised birds. Just John and me for Thanksgiving. Don't want to eat turkey for three weeks."

Art fetches it. As he wraps it, he says low, "You got my letter?"

"Yep. Those dates will work. I'll come by your place that Monday at five. If something goes wrong, call me from a pay phone. You want the full kidnapping treatment, right?"

"Oh, yes!" Smiling, Art presents me with the prettily wrapped bird. "Enjoy your holiday, sir," he says, then nods to the old lady who's sidled up behind me. "Next!"

Snow's covered the driveway by the time I get us home. I park, climb down from the truck, and stand in the snowstorm. December's cold wind cuts my face. Inside me, the fire that's driven and consumed me all my life twists and sparks and leaps a little higher.

I open the passenger door, pull off the blanket concealing my captive. Art looks up at me and grunts. "Come on, Scruff-Cub. We're home at last," I say, hauling him out. It's midwinter's early nightfall; the elderly neighbors, behind closed drapes, are watching the evening news. No one's around to see me leading toward the house a man with hands cuffed before him and black tape covering his mouth.

Half a century old this Daddybear might be, but finally I have a home-gym. No more fees to pay at the Weight Club or the YMCA. John and I have remodeled the basement, and now there's a great space for the weight set, the exercise bike, the punching bag. There's a TV (watching leather-porn is a great way to make bike-time fly), a boom box, a walk-in shower, and, on the wall, a big poster of Gerard Butler in *300*, all black beard, buff body, and warrior rage.

Tonight, though, the basement serves as dungeon. Beside the gym is the boiler room, the perfect place to keep a kidnapped cub, especially one who makes a lot of noise despite his gag. The walls are thick and windowless; he's underground, left in the dark behind a locked door. No one can hear Art's shouts and struggles, except for me, thanks to the baby monitor I bought at Wal-Mart. If the cashier had only known what uses it would be put to. I'm here in the kitchen, simmering chili and greens, frying corn fritters, sipping a martini, and relishing the muffled melodies my captive makes. If Art's hands start to go numb, all he has to mumble is the safe word "Basement" and I'll be by his side in twenty seconds. The monitor's a precautionary measure, then. It's also a pleasure. His mock-cries for help, his muted curses as he thrashes around, fighting his bonds, make me very happy.

Time to check on him. I slip the finished fritters in the microwave to heat up later, turn off the chili and greens, and descend the basement stairs. The sound of my approaching boots, he's admitted before, always makes him tense up and tremble. "Uhhh! Uhhhh!" is the gag-stifled protest I hear behind the door. Key in the lock, creaking worthy of a horror-flick. Here's my little dog-collared abductee, blinking up at me, half-blinded by the sudden shaft of light after an hour spent in total dark. He's bare-chested and barefoot, in camo pants, lying on his side on the tarp I've spread across the concrete floor. His hairy torso and belly are wrapped in taut white circles and crisscrossings of rope; his hands, biceps, and elbows are secured behind his back; his wrists and ankles are lashed together in a very tight hogtie.

There's a free-standing candelabra in the corner, *Dark Shadows*-style. I light the tapers — always liked a little romance mixed into my abduction scenes — then close the door, leaving us in the flicker of candlelight. Settling down beside him, I stroke his hair and study his roped-up torso and arms for a while in appreciative silence. Art's is the kind of body I love best, a country boy's, not a gym addict's, a physique shaped as much by good food and drink's padding as by physical exertion's muscles: arms only moderately defined, chest a compromise between hard and soft, belly a round little swell matted with golden-brown hair. I fondle that fur, a little moist from his trussed-tight struggles; I dip a finger into his navel, then stroke his goatee, sopping wet from the drool his ball gag's induced. "How you doing? All right?"

Art nods happily.

"This is what you wanted, right? Like a real kidnapping?"

Art nods again. He nuzzles my hand.

"The ball's hurting your jaw?"

Affirmative grunt. Unbuckling the strap behind his head, gently I pull the gag out. A flood of saliva follows it, oozing over his chin.

"Shit!" he gasps. "I love this! I cain't hardly move!"

Chuckling, I stretch out beside him. In between kisses, a captor's queries: "Are you warm enough? How's your circulation? Can you take a little more of this?" His lips slide over my face, nibbling and sucking. I pull off my thermal undershirt and give him a long go at my nipples, then haul out my hard-on and fuck his face. He's like a bull at a salt lick, a pig at a trough, slurping and grunting. I pull out, slap his stubble-scruffy cheeks with my dick till he's begging, then face-fuck him some more.

"I got to bake that pie, boy. Dutch apple pie with Granny Smiths, your favorite." I hump his cheeks; he puffs and snorts. "You just stay down here and work up a sweat, put up a fight. And make more noise for me. That monitor works just fine. It's a real pleasure to hear you moaning and cussing against your gag."

Pulling out again, I stand, fetch a roll of black PVC tape from the shelf of toys, and pull off a long strip. "This'll stifle those sweet cries for help," I say, falling to my knees beside him. I'm just about to press it over his pretty fur-framed lips when he says, "Uh, sir? Wait. What time is it? Herb's due to call at seven."

And so it is that, ten minutes later, I'm cross-legged on the tarp beside my hogtied Camo Cub holding his cell phone to his head while he exchanges endearments with his husband and fabricates the details of his day. There's a barely repressed tremor to his voice, a telltale straining, like a wire pulled too tight, a flag snapping in wind, something I can only hope Herb can't hear. Long-distance conversation done, I apply the tape to his mouth a little more roughly and tightly than necessary. Candles out, door locked, I head upstairs to peel apples and roll out piecrust, leaving Art helpless and hogtied in the boiler-room dark.

The sweeter the days, the faster they fly. That's my take on Virgil's line about the best days fleeing first. Soon enough our week will be done, and my boy will be gone. How much longer will he agree to meet me at the overlook? How much longer will he smile flirtatiously over the meat counter? Not long, I fear. He doesn't lie as effortlessly as I. Someday soon, he'll look at me and say, "I think Herb's onto us. I can't afford to lose him." Sometime soon, he'll say, "I don't think I can do this anymore." One day, perhaps, I'll get a note in the mail, or go by Food City, ask for him, be told he's quit, left town, up and vanished.

In the face of that, I will fill to the brim these few shared December days our timing allows. How often, after all, does anyone, especially after a certain age, feel an ardor this violent and tender, find a boy so beautiful and submissive, a boy who welcomes that ardor and matches it, if only for a little while? I want memories to serve as firewood, as stored rations, as shelter against the gray and decrepit times to come.

Art makes a pretty picture during dinner. Naked save for dog collar and jockey shorts, hands bound behind his back, he's on his knees, eating with sloppy difficulty from bowls and plates on the dining room floor. When the meal's done, I wipe his messy face, then allow him to tongue-service my cowboy boots for a bit. The bottle of Zinfindel that accompanied dinner we follow with glasses of Absente, the absinthe substitute we always share during his infrequent captivities, and some increasingly drowsy chat in the den. Hands bound before him now for maximum comfort, Art nestles on the couch beneath an afghan, his head in my lap. We watch the gas fireplace flicker and glow. Beneath the blanket, my fingers absently circle his nipples and fluff the hair over his breastbone. We talk about d John, how much we love them, how much we need the power y can't provide. We talk about Food City gossip, university politics. We watch snow fall outside the long windows, gathering on the holly bushes and the dead clematis vines.

It's almost midnight by the time I lead Art upstairs to the bedroom and strip off his briefs. From the toy bag, I fetch more lengths of rope. A few swift knots and my boy's stretched out on his back, arms and legs spread wide, tied spread eagle to the king-sized bed John and I usually share. Art moans and writhes, humping the air as I lube his hairy hole up and finger-fuck him gently. He moans louder, mumbling his thanks as I slide a lubed dildo inside him, securing it in place with a leather harness buckled around his hips and between his buttocks. I feed him apple pie and ice cream with a big spoon, dribbling a little melt here and there on his chest, armpits, and cock just to have an excuse to clean him with my tongue. He giggles and twists beneath my ministrations. "You really make me happy, Daddy," he sighs. "I'm so glad the timing worked out again. I wish we could do this more often than once I year. You really treat me fine."

"It's late," I say. "Think you can sleep like this for a while?"

"Yep," Art says. "Powerless but comfortable, my favorite bondage position. And my hole feels so damn good filled up. Thanks, sir."

"Wake me if you need to piss; there's a bucket by the bed. If you get too stiff, I'll untie you." I give him a last slurp of Absente and a long kiss, then seal his eyes and mouth with tape. Bedside lamp switched off, I tug the covers over us. Wrapping my arms around him, I rest my head on his shoulder. Outside, snow is covering the lawn, the town, the mountains. The earth is dying its annual death, but we're here together, warm and naked.

"So, I've studied that list of requests you mailed me. I have the week all planned out. You want to hear?"

"Uhhhhh huh." Art's head bounces on the pillow, pure enthusiasm.

"Tomorrow morning, after a thorough rimming, I'm going to hoist your legs over my shoulders and give you the ass-fucking of your life. You'll spend the day in those new metal wrist and ankles shackles I got from Mr. S. And that leather muzzle. Other than your bonds, this week you'll be wearing nothing but dog collar and jockstrap. I promise to keep the heat up, so you won't get cold. How's that sound?"

Art groans, "Ummmm mmmm!" I tongue a pec, nip it with my teeth, then continue.

"Let's see, what else? You'll be gulping a lot of piss this week. More hours in the boiler room, bucked and gagged some, hogtied some. The metal ball-stretcher. Tweezer clamps and alligator clamps. Clothespins covering your cock and balls. The electric fly-swatter, 'cause I know how much you love that. At some point I'm going to tie you over the preacher curl bench and rape you. Would like to paddle you black and blue, but I guess we can't leave marks, dammit."

I go on for a while, detailing scene after scene I plan to squeeze into the limits of our time together. We're both sleepy, after so much good food and drink, but now, in the barrage of these salacious details and beneath my affectionate fingertips, Art's dick grows stiff and fat. I toss back the covers, and there it is, waving its impressive heft in the air. Lassitude banished, I'm on top of him, sucking on his hard little nipples, rubbing my beard over his taped-up face. It takes only a little lube and an absurdly small number of fist-strokes before he's bucking, shouting, and shooting all over his belly fur. Straddling his waist, I cup up his cum, spread it over my own dick, and pretty soon have spattered his stubbly cheeks and goatee with my own viscous white release.

By the time I return with a washcloth moistened with warm water, Art's asleep. I wipe his face and belly clean; he mumbles, head lolling, then is out again. In the bathroom I wring the cloth out over the sink, then study my face in the mirror, in the blue glow of the nightlight. The lines across my brow are as perfectly parallel as those an expert plowman might make.

Down the dark hall I pad, to the front of the house, pinewood cold beneath my feet. Parting the curtains, I peer out over the town, gleaming below in its broad valley. Lights are vague and remote in the snow's slow falling. Draper Mountain's a black animal arching behind shifting sheets of gray. I don't know how often I'll feel this again, or if I'll ever touch another boy as beautiful, as young, furry, warm, and willing. Not often, maybe never.

If I were insane, life would be much simpler. I'd cut my initials into Art's chest with the hunting knife I keep by the bed. I'd keep him chained up in the basement and never let him loose; I'd make this mock kidnapping a reality. Maybe he'd learn to get used to it; maybe he'd finally get over Herb. Maybe, after a few weeks, he'd stop screaming for help and thank me for loving him so much.

Getting John's approval for such a move might be difficult. I smile, resting my forehead against the icy windowpane. I miss John. John will be back early next week. He'll have bought me some little present, probably something fattening and good to eat. He'll ask how my kidnapping went. I'm guessing Art loves and needs Herb the way I love and need John. I'm guessing it won't be long before Art leaves this house and never comes back.

In the bedroom, Art's snoring. I run my finger ever so lightly over his face: the line of his jaw, rough with unshaven beard-scruff; his thick sideburns and goatee; the smooth tape over his eyes and mouth. Then I light a candle, fetch what's left of my Absente, wrap myself in an extra blanket, and settle into the armchair by the bed, a chair John's grandmother once owned. Suddenly I'm not sleepy at all. Have I ever in my life stayed up all night? I don't think so. Maybe I will tonight. I'll be here for Art if he needs to piss or be untied. Tomorrow, come the dawn, I'll eat the hairy undergrowth of his ass till his taped mouth brims with begging, then push my cock up inside him where he's burning, tender, and tight, the narrow cave, the shrine where rapture dwells. Until then, hell, I'll give over florid words, sip ersatz absinthe, and watch him sleep, my pale, muscled, plump, fuzzy boy, my Scruff-Cub, stretched out like someone's suffering savior, like some immobilized and buzzard-tortured demigod chained down to a snowy mountaintop for the kind crime of giving the cold world fire.

Jeff Mann*'s books include two collections of poetry,* Bones Washed with Wine *and* On the Tongue*; a book of personal essays,* Edge: Travels of an Appalachian Leather Bear*; a novella,* Devoured*, included in* Masters of Midnight: Erotic Tales of the Vampire*; a collection of poetry and memoir,* Loving Mountains, Loving Men*; and a volume of short fiction,* A History of Barbed Wire*, winner of a Lambda Literary Award. He teaches creative writing at Virginia Tech in Blacksburg, Virginia.*

Persian Justice

Jay Starre

Marduk was outwardly congenial but inwardly cautious. Cousin to the Emperor himself and accustomed to immense power, the Persian Satrap of Media feared little.

Goliath stood before him as he lounged on his low couch amidst embroidered cushions and exotic furs. His large thighs sprawled wide in a gesture of blatant invitation. Beneath his crimson gown his prick rose in a turgid column of lust.

"How may I serve Your Highness?"

Goliath's voice purred, although there was an underlying rumble that only added to Marduk's suspicions.

"That remains to be seen. If your Master, the Prince of Damascus, has provided you with sufficient silver shekels to dispense, then we are on good terms."

Marduk's large arms spread across the back of his couch, adding to the image of openness he contrived to portray. With his bearded lips curled in a smile, the Satrap repositioned his hips slightly, thrusting up with his crotch just enough to call attention to the thick bulge rising up beneath the folds of his silken gown.

The Phoenician ambassador's golden orbs flickered quickly over that obvious bulge as he dropped his eyes in outward submission and proffered a flourishing bow.

"My Prince has indeed provided me with a substantial fund of shekels. I offer you his submission, as well as my own."

"Ah, then come forward. Kneel at my feet and I will accept that submission."

The moment was fraught with tension. Marduk judged this giant brute as both wily and dangerous. Those qualities were not unsuitable for an ambassador. But criminals, and assassins, also boasted those merits.

Goliath strode forward with eyes downcast, as cautious as the King before him. Yet he knelt without hesitation between the Median's widespread thighs. Bowing his head, his face hovered over Marduk's lap.

The Satrap reached out and placed a large palm over the kneeling ambassador's scalp, exerting just the slightest downward pressure. Crowned by a curling mass of sandy-brown hair, the burly Phoenician's face lowered further as that palm urged.

This moment was crucial. Would the so-called ambassador comply, would he resist, would he produce a weapon from the hidden folds of his gown? Marduk waited, outwardly calm, inwardly prepared for action.

The honey-gold eyes darted upward for one quick glance at the Satrap's placid features, then returned to stare into the lap so close. There was no mistaking the thick bulge tenting that crimson gown. In fact the column of flesh beneath actually jerked and rose toward the hovering visage.

He capitulated, face dropping, bearded mouth nuzzling the firm outline of Satrap prick awaiting his attentions.

"Ah ... so you offer your Prince's obeisance readily. That is fine. Now, you may show Us your own submission."

The husky voice oozed arrogance yet the Satrap was by no means shedding his caution. Not at all. Even as the bearded lips in his lap gently massaged prick through crimson silk, and the ambassador's large hands slid around his ankles and began to lift his gown, he remained vigilant.

Goliath's palms as they slithered up the Satrap's firm, hairy calves, were muscular and calloused, not typical of a politician who might spend his days in soft living, but not entirely out of character either. Many a nobleman engaged in manly pursuits such as chariot driving, archery, wrestling and even at times a warrior's grim business.

The hands lifted Marduk's robe, revealing husky thighs coated in silken black hair, fleshy but powerful from the Satrap's own active lifestyle. The robe slid higher to reveal the plump seed sack lying on the couch between those large thighs, and the base of the mighty shank the King claimed.

"Taste my stem. Reveal your talents."

The drawled command was emphasized by more pressure on Goliath's scalp. The palm over it directed the bearded face toward the prick now displayed. The ambassador's fingers tangled in the folds of crimson silk as he pushed farther upward. Marduk's entire lower body, solid and coated in silken black fur was revealed.

Pink lips gaped wide as mouth engulfed the bobbing crown of purple prick. Both men emitted rumbling moans, their barrel chests equal in size and power. Their contest was far from over — even as the ambassador began a noisy suckling, and the Satrap offered a curling smirk as he stared down at the massive brute kneeling between his thighs.

"Prepare the Spear for its coming work. Next, you will offer me your anal submission to cement our filial accord."

The face in his lap bobbed in acknowledgment, the giant body leaning forward, the knees sliding apart in a gesture of obedience. The ambassador wore a knee-length robe of deepest emerald, now stretching taut across powerful buttocks above calves coated in fair hair and bulging with muscle.

Goliath, smacking his lips as he waxed enthusiastic over the drooling knob in his mouth, outwardly exhibited not only submission, but apparent eagerness to comply with the Satrap's command.

One of his hands disentangled itself from Marduk's robe and whipped around to grasp the hem of his own. He yanked upward, exposing burly thighs and the fleshy expanse of his lush posterior. Gobbling prick deeper, past his tonsils and into the tight confines of his throat, he gurgled as he actually wriggled that large ass, and then dropped his big hand down to finger his own deep crack in a blatant display of lewdness.

Breathing heavily as hot throat pulsed around his throbbing prickhead, Marduk heaved upward to drive deeper into the kneeling brute's mouth. Dark eyes riveted, he gazed down appreciatively at that magnificent ass between his thighs.

Now, especially, he must not lose control, even though his body vibrated with desire for the giant Goliath. He would be at his most vulnerable as he succumbed to his lust, which the kneeling giant was slurping out of him with such exquisite talent.

Just such a moment would an assassin await. Marduk danced a fine line between reveling in the delicious moment and maintaining his inner vigilance. His lust only increased as he fought that inner battle.

He continued to press downward on the top of Goliath's head as he thrust upward with his hips. He pumped that slobbering mouth, feeling the soft curls of the man's beard in his crotch, and the slippery lips massaging his shank, now close to the base as he managed to swallow nearly the entire length of that mighty Spear.

"Yes, coat my Fuck Weapon with your spittle. It is about to enter your rear sanctum. Show it to Us. Let Us see the hairy slot that awaits violation."

With a deep plunge of his mouth, the kneeling giant engulfed the Satrap's prick to the root, throat encasing it like a pulsing vice. At the same time, both his hands clamped over his own sandy-haired buttocks to grip and pull apart. In the deep valley between the plump mounds, a trail of light brown hair descended to surround a flushed and pouting anus.

Marduk leaned forward enough to see into that butt valley and appreciate the tender slot displayed. It was a sight that had his prick surging into the ambassador's tight throat as it squirted out a generous dollop of precum to coat the man's throbbing gullet.

Marduk glanced upward, tearing his eyes from that delicious sight. He needed a moment to orient himself, fearing a descent into total lust. The room, his own private chamber, was broad and open, the familiar walls covered in bold friezes of garishly painted men parading up stairs to offer obeisance to the Satrap of Media. A potent reminder of who he was and the power he wielded.

Lemon scent wafted in on the breeze from open doorways, while armed guards hovered just out of sight. Within that cool, scented breeze lingered an air of danger. He must be vigilant!

His eyes returned to that massive ass and the hole between the cheeks exhibited so delightfully. The large hands held the furry butt mounds wide apart, the lips of the hole curling apart to show the reddened flesh between. Marduk experienced a thrilled rush as the hole pouted outward, just as the mouth over his prick began to bob up and down in a sensual massage of wet heat.

He clamped his own furred thighs around the squirming hips, holding the kneeling ambassador immobile, one hand on his scalp, the other now on the small of his back above the hem of his rope and on the place where spine terminated and crack began.

What did this man want? In the audience chamber amidst a score of other ambassadors and petitioners, the tall ambassador had requested a private audience, hinting of secret dealings that would be of great interest to the Satrap. Marduk had been suspicious, but intrigued. Now here they were.

It was time to hear of this secret message. His fingers, curled in the sandy locks of the slurping Goliath, tugged upward, pulling the bearded lips off his prick with a juicy smack.

"Tell Us what it is you seek, or offer."

The honey-gold orbs gazed up into Marduk's hooded black eyes. There was no hesitation as the drool-coated lips moved in a sibilant whisper. "My Prince seeks Your aid. He knows You have the ear of the Glorious Emperor. Would You intercede for him against the Israelites? I am authorized to present You with a generous fee. Very generous."

Perhaps true. Perhaps not. Marduk chose to smile as he lifted the giant ambassador by the hair, pulling him up so that they were face to face. "Let Us taste of your generosity first before Our decision is made."

He pulled the wet lips to his and forced his tongue between them. At the same time, his free hand thrust up between Goliath's furry thighs. An enormous fuck tool twitched between his fingers as the giant moaned around the Satrap's stabbing tongue.

Marduk released the substantial prick and thrust lower, quickly seizing and squeezing the plump seed sack before releasing that and probing further — up between the splayed thighs, into the heated ass-crack where he discovered a quivering, fur-rimmed hole.

Goliath had both hands on his buttocks, pulling them wide apart as he'd been ordered earlier. Now he squirmed around the fingers suddenly stroking the lips of his fuckhole. His hands gripped the hem of his gown and pulled upward, yanking the robe toward his armpits, revealing almost all of his lush body for the Satrap's perusal.

Marduk pulled the mouth off his, fingers tangled in scalp still. "Now is the time for you to reveal your anal talents. You will be naked as you squat over my Spear."

The command was hissed in Goliath's face, hot breath in his nostrils. Eyes locked for a heartbeat before the ambassador's dropped and he struggled to his feet to tear off his gown.

No hidden dagger came forth as the robe was yanked over Goliath's head and he became entirely naked. He spun around at the same time, bending over and squatting as he had been commanded.

Marduk surveyed the nude body. Large and muscular, sandy fur coated the buttocks and thighs, while the broad back was smoother. The massive arms, stretched behind as Goliath gripped his own buttocks with big hands to spread them, were also coated in that light brown fur.

He had the look of a Greek to him, which did little to allay Marduk's suspicions. Sworn enemies of the Persians, and often hired as mercenaries-and assassins. Even the Greeks of Ionia under the Emperor's rule were in constant rebellion.

But then the hairy buttocks descended and that pink hole found its target. The moist lips grazed the crown of Marduk's prick, settled on it and began to rub and tease. He gasped, grudging admiration at the talent displayed, his spit-coated prick-head pulsing and oozing with delight.

The teasing massage continued as the large butt-cheeks hovered over Marduk's lap. The hole itself pouted around the blunt knob, anal lips actually caressing it in a slippery massage. Marduk groaned and thrust upward, unable to control himself.

That big ass descended at that precise moment, encasing and swallowing the entire fat crown in a greedy gulp.

Both men grunted together. Pulsing hole engulfed cock. Without hesitation, that hole opened up to swallow more cock. The brutish ambassador slowly sat on the Satrap's lap, gulping up prick until he had taken it all.

"Yes. Yes," Marduk groaned.

"Yes Master. My hole is Yours," Goliath moaned.

There was no indication of falsity in the moaning, grunting impalement that followed. The giant squatted over Marduk's lap, rising and falling as he fucked his own pulsing hole over that mighty tool. Head down, giant body heaving and muscles straining, he humped and writhed with steady enthusiasm.

Marduk ripped off his own gown over his head, tossing it aside. Entirely nude now, his heavily furred body pressed into the squatting giant in his lap. He reached around and attacked the mighty chest, teasing the furringed nipples with tugging and pinching, as Goliath emitted little gasps and thrust out his chest against that assault.

One of the Satrap's long-fingered hands dropped down to seize Goliath's drooling prick and pump it. His giant body jerked, hairy buttocks clenching around prick up his hole, chest out-thrust, cock sliding between the fingers gripping it. Sandy curls soaked in sweat, head tossing, moans and grunts constant, Goliath flopped and writhed in seemingly total capitulation.

Yet, Marduk required more. "On your back, legs spread and hole available for Our use!"

The snarled command contained no measure of tolerance. The giant Goliath must obey and obey instantly. He did.

Bounding up off the prick he had ridden so zealously, the big brute managed to whirl and leap in a display of athleticism that brought back every bit of Marduk's suspicion. Still, the ambassador offered total obedience, flopping onto his back beside the Satrap on his couch, lifting his own hirsute thighs and pulling them back to his chest.

His furry hole, slathered with spit and sweat, gaped open for Marduk's inspection. The Satrap crawled up between those splayed thighs, potent prick rearing, purple and engorged. He aimed it at that pulsing slot and slowly began to feed it to the grunting ambassador.

Marduk leaned into the uplifted thighs, feeling the silken down of light brown hair against his own dark fur. His prick slithered into heated fuck channel, stretching the convulsing ass-lips and torrid fuck channel just beyond. He watched as his giant tool slowly disappeared within the churning pit.

With deliberate savagery, he began to pummel the gaping hole. To his satisfaction, Goliath reared up with his mighty buttocks to take the pounding prick inside. His honey-gold eyes stared up between his own splayed thighs into the dark orbs of the Satrap who violated him.

Marduk fucked relentlessly, slamming into Goliath's asshole. He locked eyes with the man as he gored him with his thick weapon. Goliath bit his pink lip and moaned, sweat dripping down his flushed face. His own cock flagged momentarily when the powerful fuck began, but then reared back up defiantly as the pounding continued.

"You may stroke it. I will fuck a load from your seed sack. You will give me your spunk as a token of your submission."

The words were practically spit out as Marduk slammed his burly hips forward against the upraised buttocks of his victim. His hands gripped the brute's ankles, controlling and pinning him beneath his sweating bulk.

Goliath dared not look away as the Satrap held his gaze and rammed him with prick. He pumped his own drooling tool and shook from head to toe, bent over backward, thighs splayed and hole wide open.

Helplessly, the giant ambassador flailed beneath the Satrap. Prick slithered in and out with slurping squishes. Hole pouted and clung to purple shank, massaged and teased relentlessly. Prostate mashed and sensitive anal ring burning with friction, Goliath could no longer hold out against the relentless assault.

"I am coming! Master, I am giving You my seed!"

The blurted words were followed immediately by a spewing eruption. The slit in Goliath's pink-crown gaped open as semen sprayed upward in a violent spattering.

Grinning with cruel satisfaction, Marduk pounded his prick home, each thrust causing another spray of seed to erupt from the fucked ambassador's cock. At the same time, Goliath's hole went into clamping convulsions around the thrusting weapon violating it.

The honey-gold eyes went out of focus, the lush lips gaped and the sandy-curled head tossed as great moans erupted from the ambassador's chest. Marduk chose that moment to plant his own seed.

"You will take My load. You will surrender to My command."

Cum spewed deep into the violated ambassador's churning innards. The look in his eyes was of total capitulation.

Breathless moments followed as the pair enjoyed a mutual orgasm, their heaving bodies slowly growing still. Marduk finally released the ambassador and moved away to lie back on his couch, quiet as he awaited the man's next move.

Goliath rose on shaky thighs. Naked still, he stood before the Satrap, exhibiting for the first time a sense of unease, and lack of confidence., Finally, as Marduk refused to offer him any leeway, he managed to speak …

"You know, don't You?"

"Yes. But be not afraid. I offer you more than your life. I offer you service. In My employ."

The eyes roamed up and down the sweaty Satrap's magnificent body. They settled on the potent prick now rising again from the furry lap. A smile began to curve the pink lips.

"Ah, yes. Now that is an offer I cannot refuse."

He came forward and knelt again between the spread thighs. His mouth came down. He suckled his new Master's Spear.

Marduk sighed. He was content. Goliath would be his.

For a time, at least.

A Canadian, ***Jay Starre*** *has pumped out hot stories for dozens of gay men's men anthologies including* Bear Lust, Rough Trade, *and* Special Forces. *His two gay erotic novels are Th*e Erotic Tales of the Knights Templar *and* Lusty Adventures of the Knossos Prince.

Bears and Their Toys

Jonathan Cohen

Okay, so Sam and I were sitting in our shared office at *National Bear Magazine* when the package arrived, addressed to me. I wasn't all that worried; the only feedback I ever got on my columns was the occasional twenty-page email and the subscription to *Elle* Magazine. I felt confident that my positive outlook, sunny disposition, and bronzer could help me weather anything my readers might throw at me. Then I opened the box.

Inside was a miniature bear (a real, two-legged one), about 11 inches high, with a beard, flannel, and tiny cowboy boots. The tag on the doll read "Bearbie."

"My God!" Sam said. "It's the final commercialization of the bear movement!" Then, after a second, "Give it to me! I want to play with it!"

We took turns examining Bearbie. According to the box, he came with "realistic simulated beard and chest hair flocking," two outfits (jeans/plaid shirt/leather vest, and jeans/leather shirt/plaid vest), and was anatomically correct.

Sam pulled open the fly of the microscopic 501s. "He looks like your first boyfriend — only smaller."

"That was a medical condition!" I shot back. Then I discovered the pull string on Bearbie's back and gave it a good yank.

"Monogamy is hard!" it said in a tinny voice. Sam and I just looked at each other.

That's when Smokey appeared at the door. As Editor-in-Chief of *NBM*, he had to have something to do with this. He grinned. "So, what do you think?"

"I'm speechless," I said. Sam pulled the string again, and Bearbie said "I'm sorry, I don't have the rent money this month."

"We're betting the farm on this one," Smokey announced. "A massive campaign in print and on the Web. I figure we can sell 10,000 of these a year." He looked at us slyly. "Market research says that this will appeal to bears' nesting and collecting instincts. As well as the fact that every bear got to have what everyone else has."

"That is *such* crap," Sam sneered, grabbing the Bearbie out of my hands and stroking the simulated flocking.

Smokey turned to go. "One last thing, Carey," he said. "Say something about it in your column. Something positive. Maybe you could go out on a date with it or something. Your boyfriend's still recovering from that depilation, right?"

After he'd left, I looked into Bearbie's devil-may-care eyes and sighed. "I know who'd love it," I said, shaking my head. "Richard."

Sam was already busy surfing the Web for porn. "Who's that?"

I put the tiny hat with BEAR! written on it on Bearbie's head. "The guy I'm dating this week. He's sweet, really he is, but just a bit dull. He collects things."

"Dildos?" Sam asked, momentarily distracted from www.ourfirstbeartime.com.

"Spoons, bottle caps, Hummel figurines." I sighed. "It's our one-and-a-half date tonight, and if we don't have bed sex, I'm going to have to dump him."

"You've had half a date with the guy and you haven't had sex yet?" Sam asked, incredulous.

"Sex in the park doesn't count," I said. "The true measure of a bear is when he invites you into his bed."

And, I reflected that evening, it was so true. When a bear is over at your place, or in the bushes, or a sex club, he's not usually expressing his whole sexual nature. It's only when you slip between his satin sheets that you discover what he's really made of.

When I eased myself into his flannel sheets, I discovered a rope. A cable, really.

"Uh, looks like you left this out," I said uneasily, holding it up. It seemed a bit greasy.

Richard gave me a devil-may-care grin that reminded me of Bearbie. "Can I interest you in a little … kink?" he asked.

Richard was naughty in that little-cub kind of way, one of the Gen-X bears who was still between university and real life at the age of 28. I looked at the rope and shrugged. "Sure, go ahead," I said. "I have to write a column about something this week."

The next morning, I was gingerly poking pushpins into Bearbie when Sam came in and did a double-take. "You look like you've been folded in half," he said, giving me a shoulder massage. "Did his Hummel figurine collection fall on you?"

I finished my voodoo on Bearbie and sighed. "Last night, *I* was the fully-posable action figure." I showed Sam a rough patch on my chin. "I think Richard rubbed off some of my simulated flocking."

"You're such an amateur," Sam said, sitting down at his desk and comforting Bearbie. "When I was your age, I'd been branded as a bad boy. Not to mention property of the Lazy-Q Ranch."

I groaned as my muscles shifted into a new chiropractic position. "The problem is, I like Richard, but I can't take any more of this sex. I'm going to have to dump him after all."

"Screw that, dear," Sam said. "Just wear him out. Give him the B&D, S&M, J&B night of his dreams and he'll be vanilla for the rest of the week, or until the relationship ends, whichever comes sooner."

"I don't follow your reasoning," I said.

"The only reason he wants kinky rough sex with you," Sam explained patiently, "is because you don't want it. Once you show that you do want it, he won't want it anymore, and you can have the sexless relationship that every bear couple eventually ends up as."

Maybe it was the massive painkillers, but Sam's position made sense. I was combing Bearbie's simulated flocking when the doll writhed in my hands. I dropped it and leapt out of my chair, then groaned and rubbed my back. "Bearbie just groped me!" I said.

Sam rolled his eyes. "Did you take one of my blue pills, or one of my red ones? Because if you took the blue one …"

At that point Bearbie spoke on his own, and we both shut up. "Oh yeah!" it said in a mini-butch voice. "You like that big bear dick, don'tcha?"

Then I glanced over at Sam's computer. His browser was showing the home page of Mason Stone, bearporn star. There was a video clip of Mason jerking himself off and saying "You like that big bear dick, don'tcha?"

I reached over and shut the browser down. Bearbie stopped moving. Then I started the browser again, and it went to Mason Stone's site (Sam had set it as the default). "Oh yeah," Bearbie shrilled suddenly, "Take it all!"

I stormed into Smokey's office with Bearbie and slammed it down on his desk. "Careful," Smokey said. "Those things cost over 50 cents to make."

"You're going to use these things to subliminally influence bears across the country into buying Mason Stone's latest porn video!" I said accusingly.

"Well, duh," Smokey said. "Bearbie is keyed to respond to Mason's vocal frequencies. Once the geek bears figure it out, they'll be falling all over each other to buy it."

I shook a finger at him. "You'll never get away with it! Bears will never fall for a clever marketing scheme designed to make them buy more bear-related merchandise!"

Silence.

"Oh fuck it," I said. "I'm going to get one of Sam's red pills."

The next day, I was in even worse shape. I just glared at Sam when he entered the office and kept sticking pushpins into Bearbie. "I take it the sex overload thing didn't pan out," he said.

"Not in the slightest," I said through gritted teeth. "Now Richard wants to introduce me to his sling. And something to do with bendy straws! This has gone way too far."

Sam rescued Bearbie just as I pushed a pushpin right into its crotch. "Let me take care of Richard," he said. "I'll wear him out for you."

I considered this. On the one hand, it meant dating a bear I couldn't have sex with. On the other hand, Sam would keep supplying me with red pills. "Go ahead," I said wearily. "Just make sure he doesn't enjoy it."

That night, I sat alone in my apartment and watched a rerun of *The Nanny* while I waited for news from Sam. The phone rang just as I was about to go to sleep. It wasn't Sam, but Charlie. "You have to come down to the hospital, right away!"

I eased myself out of the chair. "What is it? What's happened?"

"Richard's in the hospital!" Charlie said. "They're trying to extract some kind of doll from his butt!"

Even in my shock, I could smell a product liability lawsuit. When I arrived at the hospital, Richard had his ass in the air and was resting on a pillow. Sam looked half-guilty, half-defiant.

"You were using Bearbie for sex play?" I asked in horror.

"Well," Sam said, "everything was going fine until Bearbie freaked out. It started shaking and vibrating inside Richard, and finally it got stuck there."

Then I got a horrible idea, a wonderful horrible idea. "Were you watching TV at the time?" I asked, grinning despite myself.

Richard looked at Sam, then at me. "Well, as a matter of fact, we were ..."

We all looked up at the TV monitor above the bed, which showed the only person in the world whose vocal frequencies matched Mason Stone's. And that, I thought, would be enough to sink the Bearbie scheme permanently.

Once again, Fran Drescher had saved the day.

Jonathan Cohen *is author of the novel* Bear Like Me, *scheduled to be reissued by Bear Bones Books.*

"The Norsemen Are Coming!"

Jesse Monteagudo

"The Norsemen are coming!"

The morning that I heard those words, I was working in the vineyard, tending the grapes that we use to make communion wine. Tending the vineyard is hard but satisfying work; one that keeps me healthy and out of doors. It also gives me time to meditate, which is more than I could do if were tending the flocks (our Monastery's other source of income). The other monks usually leave me along while I do my work, which is fine by me.

The Monastery of St. Benedict of León sits on a rock that faces the Northern Sea, in the Kingdom of León. Except for the occasional Basque fishing vessel, most of our commerce is conducted with the nearby peasants or with agents of the King of León in nearby Asturias. Since our monastery was founded over a century ago, the Monks of León have devoted our lives to the love of God and the service of humanity, tending our flocks and our vineyards and preserving the ancient writings that would have otherwise been lost. Though the land around the monastery is prone to occasional earth tremors, it is a good place to live in, even for those us who have taken vows of poverty, chastity, and obedience.

There is not much to say about myself. I was born the son of illiterate peasants, who to this day make a living by tilling the fields. The last of many children, I grew up as the runt of the litter: short, stocky, swarthy and hairy. Unlike my brothers, I was never interested in a peasant's life: marrying early, having children, or tilling the fields. From an early age I was drawn to the monastic life, and to a community of men dedicated to God, humanity and one another. When I joined the Monastery of St. Benedict of

León at the age of 18, our Blessed Abbot, Padre Pio, saw in me a capacity for words and communication. Under his guidance, I learned to read and write and to appreciate the sacred manuscripts in the Monastery library. Since then, Padre Pio appointed me the monastery scribe, entrusted to write our history: "You have a way with words, Brother Mauro. Chronicle our history for future generations." And so I did. I also keep a secret journal, which I hide under a rock in the vineyard. May God forgive me for this sin of vanity.

"The Norsemen are coming!" cried the watchman, startling me our of my morning meditation. Leaving the vineyard to its own devices, I ran towards the grazing fields where Brother Andrés scrambled to collect the flocks. Like myself a young monk in the Order of St. Benedict, Brother Andrés was a pleasant monk, not too smart but strong as an ox. It was Brother Andrés's task to tend to the flocks whose wool, like our wine, provided our Monastery with revenue. Though tending to his flock was a task that Brother Andrés would gladly do by himself under ordinary circumstances, saving it from invaders required some assistance. As I helped Brother Andrés drive the sheep to safety, I nervously gazed out towards the ocean, waiting for a northern ship to hover over the horizon.

"Where are the Norsemen?" I asked Brother Andrés.

"They will be here soon enough," he replied. "The watchman, Brother Gardo, saw a Northern ship just over the horizon, and Padre Pio received a message this morning from the Monks of Santa Cecilia, a few leagues down the coast. Their home was ravaged by the Norsemen, perhaps by the very same ship that threatens us today, and they barely escaped with their lives. I pray we do not suffer their fate," he added, as he wiped off the sweat with his robe. Like myself, Brother Andrés was short and stocky and covered with thick black hair which made him sweat a lot when nervous. "I pray that the King's troops will do the right thing and come to save us from our ruin."

"What can the King and his troops do," I said, "when they are barely able to police their own lands?" Since the heathen Moors conquered the Kingdom of Granada to the south, the Kingdom of León remained isolated against the Northern Sea, helplessly alone against the invading forces from the Northern Sea. For a while the Empire of the Franks protected us from alien invaders but now the Franks themselves were gone and we were left alone to fend to ourselves. For years we have been waiting for the Norse invasion to come; ever since a band of Norsemen burned the sacred shrine of Sant'Iago de Compostela. As a rule the Norsemen only attack during the summer, when the waters are warm and the winds blow from the north. Now it was summer, and the Norsemen were only a few leagues away. We could be next.

"Here they come!" shouted Brother Gardo from his tower, as a Norse ship crept over the horizon. Larger than any of the Basque fishing vessels, the vessel was almost 100 feet long, with sails as tall as our church steeple. A ferocious dragon's head adorned the ship's front. But not even a dragon could match the fierce warriors who manned the ship: tall, husky, hairy, blond Norsemen clad in furs. Above each warrior's head was a horned helmet, a symbol of Viking strength. They were obviously a renegade group; just a dozen errant Norsemen who were eager for booty of their own, apart from their countrymen. Even so, these men were armed to the teeth, and seemed strong enough to subdue a hundred or so terrified monks. We had no time to lose.

Fortunately, we had a plan. "To the church!," I shouted at Brother Andrés, who was already ahead of me. As we ran towards the monastic church, Padre Pio rang the church bells, warning the neighborhood of the impending crisis. From all directions monks and villagers ran towards the church; some carrying their small children and others their aged parents. As we nervously huddled inside the church, we could hear the savage pagan ship touch land and its warriors disembark. At best, our flocks and vineyards were in deadly danger. At worst, so were we.

As men of peace, the Monks of St. Benedict of León did not own weapons. But we were willing to lay down our lives to protect our own and our community. As the women, children and old men huddled in the background, we joined the men of the village to put up a barrier inside the door of the church, to delay the Norse warriors' entrance for as long as possible. As the Norsemen tried to break down the door, I prayed to Sant'Iago de Compostela and St. Benedict for a miracle, hoping that they would protect us from these godless marauders.

All of a sudden, as in the days of old, the earth shook and trembled, shaking the church to its core. Miraculously, most of the monks and villagers survived the tremors, for the damage was mainly in the front of the church. The Norsemen were not so lucky. As we crept outside, we saw them all spread motionless upon the ground, struck by the church steeple which had fallen upon them. All 12 of them appeared to be dead.

"Praise God," shouted Padre Pio, as we all cheered our unexpected fortune. We knew that this was not the end, and that Norse ships would once again endanger our shores. But for now, we were safe. As we gathered our dead for burial, I could not help but feel sorry for the brave Norsemen who lied at my feet, for they possessed an unusually manly beauty, like husky blond angels from heaven.

"One is still alive!," shouted Brother Andrés, as one of the fallen warriors moaned into consciousness. He was a tall, beefy Norseman, about my age, with long golden hair and beard. Like the Hercules of pagan myth, he had powerful arms and thighs; as well as broad shoulders, chest and belly that the furs could barely hide.

"Kill him!," shouted one of the villagers as some of the others shouted in agreement. Though I could understand their anger, I would not allow their vengeance to proceed. There was a reason why God kept this Norseman from killing us, just as he prevented Abraham from killing his son Isaac so long ago. As holy men, it is our duty to serve all of mankind, even the savage Norse I was determined to save this man's body and, perhaps eventually, his soul.

"You can't kill him!," I pleaded. "He has done nothing. If God kept him from their fate," I said, pointing to the Norse corpses nearby, "it is for a reason. And it is our duty to bury the dead and heal the living."

"Oww!," moaned the powerful Norse, in a voice so strong that it almost scared us out of our robes. As I knelt beside him, he proceeded to utter what seemed to us to be a string of unintelligible sounds. I tried to listen to his words, trying to make sense of what he saying, knowing all too well that I knew nothing of the Norse language (or vice versa). While everyone stared, I pointed to myself and gave out my name, "Mauro."

"Olf," said the Norseman, nodding in agreement. At least we knew our names. Feeling his head, I noticed he was warm and asked Brother Andrés to bring me some cooling water. While Olf drank the water that was given to him by Brother Andrés, I consulted with Padre Pio.

"This man needs rest and recovery," I said, as I got on my feet. "Is there any place in the monastery that we can lodge him in?"

"Yes, with you," said the Abbot, who was a bit annoyed. "The monastery is full to capacity, and we do not have room for injured Norsemen.

However, as the monastery's scribe, you have your own private cell, near the library. I assign you the task of taking care of your Norseman, at least until he's fully recovered."

"May God's will be done," I said. Though I did have a cell to myself, a privilege that was otherwise enjoyed by only Padre Pio himself, it seemed too small to accommodate a Norse giant. On the other hand, my cell was located on the far side of the monastery, by the library, which would allow Olf to moan and groan without bothering the other monks. Brother Andrés and I lifted Olf and carried him over to my cell which, like the rest of the monastic house, was blessedly undamaged by the recent earth tremor. Though Olf moaned and groaned in discomfort as we carried him, he managed to fall asleep by the time Brother Andrés and I laid him in my bed. As I feared, Olf was so big that he filled my bed, leaving me without a place to lay my head.

"You may share my bed tonight, Brother Mauro," said Brother Andrés, always helpful. Though I was aware of Brother Andrés's love for me, I never saw him as more than a friend and brother. Still, I appreciated his assistance and his company. But I would not sleep with him.

"We can not do that," I replied. "But thank you anyway." By the Code of St. Benedict, young monks are not allowed to share a bed. On the other hand, it was quite proper for a monk to share his sleeping quarters with a wounded man, even if the man was a pagan Viking warrior. After the disappointed Brother Andrés left me, I turned to make sure that Olf was quietly asleep. Once I determined that he was, I left my cell in order to complete my daily chores.

Later that evening I returned to my cell, with a pail of clear water and a cloth. Though bathing was not the custom in our monastery, we use it often to care for our wounded, who could benefit from the water's healing touch. Placing the pail and cloth next to my bed, I noticed that Olf was still asleep. I also noticed, once again, that he was quite beautiful.

"St. Benedict and Sant'Iago, allow me to serve this wounded man," I prayed, as I knelt besides the still sleeping Olf. Slowly and gently, I removed Olf's furs, one by one, until he was completely naked. If anything, Olf was more beautiful nude than clothed. Olf was muscular and beefy, with the body of a warrior who worked hard, fought hard, and drank strong beer. His body was covered by a mass of golden hair that was as magnificent as the furs that he wore into battle. His thighs were massive and muscular, his cock was big and thick and shielded by a thick golden foreskin, and his balls were low-hanging and full. I tried to look away, without success.

Since I became a monk, I have devoted my life to the love of God and the service of mankind. I willingly committed myself to a life of poverty, chastity and obedience, and did my best to avoid all temptations. Now temptation starred at me in the face. I have heard somewhere that the Norsemen worshiped the phallus. Olf's stiff prick was like a golden idol, one that seemed more real to me than the saints to who I prayed each day. Old pagan books in the monastery library — forbidden to the monks but not to the monastery scribe — described the beauty of the ancient gods. This heroic Viking was a match for Jupiter, Apollo, or Mars.

I stood up. Now back on my feet, I removed my robe. Since monks are not allowed to have a mirror in their cells, I gazed at my own reflection in the pail of water. Though my body was adequate enough to do the hard work required of a young monk, I never thought of myself as beautiful. I was short, stocky, swarthy and very hairy. A mop of dark hair covered my head, a dark beard covered my face, and a dark fur covered most of my body. I was just the son of illiterate peasants from León, not a magnificent Norseman. My own cock was small and thick and covered with a thick dark foreskin. I was told by my father and my brothers that I was ugly, and I believed it, even when Brother Andrés insisted otherwise. Would I be worthy of the beauty that lied at my feet? Through all of this, Olf remained asleep, oblivious to my dilemma.

I got back on my knees. I began to give Olf a cloth bath, washing away from his body the sweat and the grime. As I cleaned Olf's hairy, husky, muscular body, I prayed that I would not be tempted by it, all the time wanting desperately to hold it and kiss it and love it. As if to taunt my deepest fears, Olf's prick suddenly became hard — and inviting. Though the monastic rules forbade the young monks from touching each other, or even themselves, it surely would be no sin for me to touch Olf's hard cock, if it was part of a cleaning. I pushed apart Olf's massive thighs to take a closer look at the treasure within.

In our monastic tradition we talk about performing labors of love. Cleaning Olf's hard cock and low-hanging balls was truly a labor of love, one that I accomplished with all the care and devotion that I could muster. Once cleaned, Olf's genitals were even more inviting, and I could no longer resist. Olf's cock and ball deserved my oral devotion. But I proceeded quietly, for I feared that Olf would awaken.

First I worked on Olf's golden balls, licking one low-hanger and then the other before sucking them both. I then took Olf's stiff dick in my mouth, licking the shaft with my tongue while thrusting it deep down my hungry throat. To my surprise, my own cock reacted to my selfless labor of love, getting hard without being touched. My body also took on a life of its own, shifting around so that my stomach sat on top of Olf's burly chest and his head faced my hairy ass. Which is the first thing Olf saw as he suddenly work up.

"Hey!" Olf shouted in own language, startling me. For a moment, I feared for my life, for a Norseman's anger is well-known. However, Olf had other plans in mind. Instead of tearing me apart, Olf pushed my head back towards his cock, urging me to continue sucking. I obediently took Olf's cock in my mouth again, sucking it and licking it with all my might. Though Olf remained in a prone position, he managed to get his hands on my buttocks, pushing them apart to reveal my inviting asshole within.

As I continued to worship Olf's phallus, Olf wet a finger in the water pail and pushed it deep inside my hairy asshole. An erotic thrill coursed through my body as Olf's finger probed deeply inside my hole. When I was still a boy, I discovered my ass to be a source of great pleasure. Even as a monk, I would sometimes massage my rectum with my fingers, or with another instrument. Now for the first time ever, another man was giving me anal pleasure. Though part of me wanted this sinful ecstasy to stop, the rest of me wanted it to go on. And so we did. I continued to suck Olf's cock and Olf continued to loosen my ass, first with one finger, then with two, and finally with three. Meanwhile my own hard cock, with a mind of its own, pushed mightily against Olf's muscular chest. Only my room's distance from the other cells kept the monks from discovering our mutual pleasure.

Unlike me, Olf was not inexperienced in the love of men. He knew what he wanted and what I needed. With a mighty roar, Olf rose from the bed, throwing me on the ground with my legs in the air. Now in command, Olf aimed his phallus at my helpless but willing asshole, now lubricated and stretched to capacity. Pain and pleasure combined as Olf thrust his cock inside me, fucking me mercilessly again and again. Not being satisfied with possessing my ass, Olf took over my nipples, chewing one tit and then the other and giving me a pleasure I did not know was possible. Meanwhile, my own hard cock, still hard, pushed against Olf's brawny chest. It wasn't long before the two of us reached the point of no return. Olf and I exploded at once, as our orgasms (my first!) sent his semen deep inside of my ass and my own splashed all over his chest.

With all passion spent, I felt fearful. I had done the unthinkable, having succumbed to the love of another man for the first time in my life. And what was Olf thinking? Having experienced unexpected pleasure with me, would Olf now react with anger? Or will he reject me, seeing for the first time my short, husky, swarthy and hairy body? Olf relieved my fears by pulling me towards him, taking me in his strong arms, and kissing me. Olf also smiled at me, for the first time. (So did I.) For the rest of the night, the two of us slept together in my narrow bed, happy and content.

Since that fateful day and night Olf the Viking became a part of our monastic community. Now fully recovered, Olf learned our language, was baptized, and eventually joined our monastic order as Brother Juan. And while there is always much work to do, and many rules to obey, Brother Juan and I manage to find times to be alone together. And thus I conclude this chapter in the secret journal, which I preserve under a rock in the vineyard of the Monastery of St. Benedict of León. I hope future generations will discover this journal and learn what happened to us on the day and the night that the Norseman came.

Jesse Monteagudo *is a freelance writer who lives in South Florida with his husbear and many friends. He writes articles, interviews and reviews for a variety of gay print and online publications and has contributed gay erotic fiction to over two dozen anthologies.*

Everyone's a Winner

S. Bear Bergman

Some people say it happens when their eyes lock across a crowded room, but for us it was lust at fifty paces. Striding across a field, running late after leading a bondage class, I wasn't halfway to the group of men gathered to talk about creating community when I looked up from the path and right at him. Granted, who's hot and who's not is a subjective question, but this stocky, strong-looking bear with big paws and a bright smile was exactly my type. And he was looking right at me, smiling that smile. My cock jumped in my baggy shorts, and I willed it to settle down as I took an empty seat right across from him. It declined, but the slight broadening of his grin seemed to suggest that he didn't exactly mind.

To my great surprise, I was able to participate in the conversation — the little head had, happily, not yet completely taken over. We talked for an hour in the sun about how we hoped to make our community more welcoming, more cohesive, and I was gratified to hear this handsome man making thoughtful, intelligent comments — almost as gratified as I was to notice that every time I looked at him he was looking back, the silvery strands of his salt-and-pepper hair glinting in the light. It seemed almost too much to imagine that this smart, hot man was interested in me, but I was having trouble denying the reality of it. Unless he was an Amway salesman luring me as his next mark, we appeared to be on the same page.

Any lingering doubt evaporated when the session broke. As I stood up and stretched, he walked directly over to me and held out his hand, saying "Hi, I'm Rob, and woof. I think you're really hot." I couldn't help but laugh and say "I'm Samuel, and the sentiment is entirely mutual." We talked for a bit about the run, belatedly remembering that handshakes are not, traditionally, several minutes long and finally letting go of each other's hands just as our lovers appeared, as if on cue. We made a round of introductions, everyone seemed glad to meet everyone else, and then Rob and I quietly, separately, arranged when we'd meet up with our partners later. There seemed no doubt that further conversation was in order, and though I have had my share of run hookups — all hot times with hot guys — there was something unmistakably different about the connection with Rob. The energy between us felt familiar and comfortable, but it also had its own crackle and hum, its own music. I was hot on all cylinders for this thick-necked, kind-eyed man, and anxious to stay near him a while longer.

We stood a while under a sheltering oak, taking a bit of shade and standing very close together, talking and flirting, my hand eventually coming to rest on his waist and his curling itself into my belt. We kissed, a long and luxurious kiss, and I don't mean any disrespect to anyone I have loved before or since but it was one of the best kisses of my entire life. His moustache snuck into my mouth with his tongue, and I could taste cinnamon and cigars on his breath, and his meaty hand on the back of my neck pulling me in close was warm and the skin just a little rough. I slid my hands up under his shirt, across the broad expanse of his back, and pulled him against me even more. He responded by tightening his grip on my neck further, and suddenly the kissing had an element of scuffle to it — he laughed into my mouth as he turned his hip and started trying to pull me down to the ground, and I resisted only enough to keep my feet, bumping him a little as I set them under me.

I stumbled slightly on a root and we came up for air, opening our eyes and looking at each other again. I noticed his were a pale, pale green and bright, playful. He winked and said "D'ye want to wrestle?"

I looked a little doubtful, and asked "Are you sure? You're a little out of your weight class," and patted my big belly. I was probably two inches taller and maybe fifty pounds heavier than him, by a quick guess, though a second look at his hot, muscular thighs made me revise my guess by five pounds a leg. He nodded and smiled. "Oh, yeah," he said, "if you're up for it."

I sure as hell was. I would happily have agreed to any activity that would put my body next to this hunk's, but the opportunity to actually roll around with him in the grass sent urgent signals straight to my balls. "Okay, then," I replied. "Let's do it."

We caught hands like we'd known each other for years and walked up to the natural location for such an activity, a wide flat grassy field up behind some of the cabins, away from most of the people and activities. When we got to a likely looking spot I closed the gap and kissed him again, hands on his shoulders, feeling the play of muscle under his skin and the solid shape of his neck, my hard cock agitating itself against the band of my jockstrap. I was surprised not to feel his hard-on pressing back against me, and was about to reach for it when he broke the embrace and asked, "What are the stakes?"

I raised an eyebrow. "You call it," I said, feeling confident of my advantage.

He nodded, satisfied. "Loser gets fucked. Agreed?"

With a blooming grin, I agreed cheerfully, delighted by the prospect of being balls deep inside this handsome fireplug in short order. I groped my crotch and licked my lips, making a display of my lust, and he smiled, walked right over —

— and got a heel behind mine, knocking me on my ass in a second. I scrambled, getting a hand on his neck and one behind his knee, twisting for leverage as he bulled me with his head in my ribs, fiercely. Technique, even. Fucking hot, I thought to myself as I curled and reversed, hoping to catch him off balance and use his momentum against him. It worked; my head hit his ribcage before he could right himself and I started driving him onto his back, feet scrambling for leverage in the slippery grass, one arm across his upper arm. He surprised me again, using a most counterintuitive move, collapsing flat into his back to dislodge my arm and then flipping onto his stomach, spoiling my pin. I climbed astride, bumping my now-dripping cock against his asscrack and saying "Better get used to this" in his ear, trying to get an arm under him to start levering him over while he tried to get a knee under himself to stand up. Just as he started to rise a bit, I reached around his waist to grope his crotch and started in shock - no dick! He took advantage of my surprise to rear up and knock me over, pinning me down chest to chest in the grass, legs spread wide to keep me still. Years of training focused me back on the competition, but I had sunk myself - I wasn't strong enough to shove him off such a grounded position, and he was controlling one arm with my head, making a bridge impossible. He looked down into my face, excited and anxious and short of breath and panted "Yield?"

I thrashed a little longer for good measure and then nodded, silent. He released me, and we lay on the ground, gasping, chest to chest, the smell of his sweat tangy and familiar. When I could breathe I put my hand flat on his barrel chest, feeling the play of his pecs as he breathed, and then deliberately ran it down to his crotch again, looking right into his eyes. When I got there I realized I wasn't sure I'd been right - there was definitely a hard knot, like a cock that was somehow just the head, but I wasn't sure what to make of it. I palmed it and squeezed experimentally, and the deep grunt of pleasure he made let me know that I was on more familiar ground than I might think. It didn't feel like the traditional meat-and-two-veg, but whatever we were calling it — it was definitely awake.

"You're —" I began, and he interrupted: "I'm not like the other boys."

I nodded, fumbling. "So you're not …" I trailed off.

"I'm a transman," he said, "A transman with a hard-on. A transman who just won a wrestling match."

I grinned at him. "I'm not sure you played fair," I said.

He shrugged, smiling, and replied, "Oh, poor you," and then, serious for a minute, said: "If you want to go - I mean, if this is a dealbreaker, …"

I looked at his handsome face for a minute, felt his hard thigh draped over mine, and realized my dick was still rock-hard and that my skin felt awfully good everywhere it touched his. Taking my silence for rejection, he started to pull away, but I grabbed him again and pulled him close, down against me for another kiss, chewing on his moustache and cupping the hard globes of his ass in my hands. I felt his entire body relax and then take on a whole new tension, pushing me into the ground, trapping and holding me, knees shoving my legs apart and hands curling around my wrists, holding them down.

He looked down on me again, from there, holding me down and kneeling between my legs, crotch to crotch and kissed me once, slow and deep, his tongue curling itself around mine and then fucking my mouth, filling it up until all I wanted to do was suck it. I bucked my hips against him, wanting, and he groaned into my mouth. I wanted it, even if I wasn't sure what exactly was going to happen next, and I raised my ass eagerly when his hands fumbled at my belt buckle, wanting my shorts off, kicking them away and watching in wonder as he pulled the band of my jock under my balls, making them stand up and away from my body, running a fingertip around my cockhead to catch some precum and then using it as lube to tease my asshole, which was already opening up for him. I top more often than I bottom, for sure, but I'll happily bend over for a man who can make me feel it, and this guy was making me feel it, in spades.

I must have been wandering around in my own thoughts for a moment, but came back at a cool touch against my asshole. I realized that Rob was prepared, and had gotten his hand into a rubber glove and was working a healthy dollop of lube into my hungry ass. I groaned and pushed back against his hand, stirring powerfully under his big body but being careful not to disturb his balance. He was above me, chest to chest, one hand on the ground and one working its way inside me, watching my face intently, his knees between my thighs keeping me from grinding too much. My cock ached and waved in the warming air between us; I wanted to grab it but stayed where he'd left me, hands over my head, spread out under him like a rug or a ruin. My eyes rolled back and closed as another of his fingers slipped into my warm, wanting hole, opening me further and stroking my prostate with devilish precision. My cock jumped again with every brush past that happy spot, but he kept looking right at me, kept fucking me deep and slow. His hand was alive inside me, stroking and tapping and tickling, pulling almost all the way out to flutter at the ring of my asshole before plunging back in, hard.

Gradually, so gradually, he started to pick up the pace, jolting me out of my blissful cloud of fuck reverie and into the moment. I had no idea how much of his hand was in my ass, only that it felt exactly right; I felt full of him. The warmth of the sun and the smell of the grass we were crushing made the whole thing perfect, made me so glad to be on my back in the grass on a spring day with a handsome stranger deep inside me. It was joyous, like it used to be when I was a teenager, before AIDS, when you could fall in love any afternoon for twenty minutes at a time without fear. I groaned and laughed and pushed back, offering him my ass, encouraging him to fuck me hard; I said something I only say when I'm getting fucked just right, I said "Use me, man, use my hole." And the fucker grinned like a predator cat and licked his lips and fucked me harder, deeper, adding more lube and pushing his way into me like he couldn't get enough, either.

His pistonlike pumping against my prostate started sending do-or-die messages to my cock and I reached down to grab it but he banged my hand away, groping with his other hand for the lube. He squeezed the last of the bubble onto my dick, and then skinned off his t-shirt and leaned in close, letting the warm skin and soft fur of his belly lay on my throbbing cock. It was a new kind of heaven, bucking up and down on his invading hand pumping my ass so perfectly, my cock rubbing back and forth against his hot gut, taking me incredibly close to coming. I gasped and babbled out some warning, which only made him pump harder, loving me from the inside out and making me seriously wonder why no one had ever fucked me this way before. My balls boiled, and I knew what was coming; he felt it too and leaned in to kiss me, hard — his hand up my ass, his tongue in my mouth, and my cock pumping out a hot load between our sweaty bodies. I came and came, shooting like crazy and yelling loud enough that, when the roaring in my ears subsided, I could hear cheers and applause from somewhere out of sight.

Rob let me get my legs together and relieved some of the weight on my chest, slowly coming out of my ass and snapping the glove off by our shoes. Just like when he'd pinned me we lay tangled up together on the ground, breathing hard, fingers lazing over each other's skin. I curled into the fur of his armpits, drowsing and enjoying the scent, my fingertips fiddling with his nipples and then, tentatively, tracing the scars on his chest, loving the way they were a story on his skin. My asshole throbbed appreciatively, and in my loose-limbed languor said "Damn, man," low in his ear, "you are a rock 'n' roll good time." I felt him smile, and he drawled, "You're not so bad yourself, there, mister."

I turned in his arms to look at him smiling gently, almost fondly at me; those pale green eyes alight with pleasure and the muscles of his well-developed arms standing out in relief against his skin. Incredibly, I felt my dick stir. I grinned back at him and asked: "Rematch?"

His smile widened, fast, and I felt his hips jerk just a little bit, his crotch hot against my thigh. "Same stakes?"

I nodded, smiling. That hard-working right arm of his must be tired, I reasoned, which I was already plotting how to use to my advantage. Besides which, I was more than ready to figure out how to make whatever was waiting in his shorts happy. I yanked the pouch of my jock up over my cock, half-hard again, and nudged his ribs with my head, rolling him over a bit and admiring his ass as he scrambled up, ready for another round, just like I was.

***S. Bear Bergman** is a writer, a theater artist, an instigator, a gender-jammer, and a good example of what happens when you overeducate a contrarian. Ze is also the author of* Butch Is a Noun *(Suspect Thoughts Press, 2006) and three award-winning solo performances, as well as a frequent contributor to anthologies on all manner of topics.*

A Proper Sucking

Kelvin Williams

When I was seventeen and didn't know what a Bear was, or that I was going to be the hairy-chested Bear I am today, we lived on the outer edge of a Wisconsin suburb that extended into rural areas, farms, and woods. These undeveloped properties provided nearly complete seclusion. I would go out into the woods on a clear autumn day, a cool, early summer morning, or perhaps a late winter afternoon, find a comfortable place to sit, sometimes a favorite boulder that kept me high off the ground, and I would pull out my cock and jerk off.

It wasn't just the relative privacy that I liked, but also the smell of the leaves, the mud, the trees, and the cool air that attracted me. Once I got to jacking pretty hard I would take my hand off every few minutes just to feel the cold air on my overheated cock. It felt great. Being cautious, and wary of anyone who might walk by, I only had my cock and balls exposed so that I could slip them back into my pants in a second or close my coat over my crotch. That happened occasionally but it never really worried me because I could always hear people talking from a good distance and if someone was walking alone there were always leaves crunching, twigs cracking, or puddle water splashing underfoot in plenty of time for me to compose myself.

I have never figured out how they did it — how they got so close without me knowing it — but they did.

One chilly Saturday afternoon in November I desperately needed a visit to my private boulder in the woods. I was in the middle of a good whacking, pulling the quarter inch of skin I could manage in short strokes up over the edge of my circumcised cock head; faster and slower, then faster and slower, with my eyes shut and my head back.

In my imagination I was about to get my faced fucked by my favorite high school jock, Nick Cipriano. Nick barely even knew who I was. I'd seen Nick wresting, swimming, playing soccer and running track. He was a stocky five feet, six inches tall, short trunk, thick legs, with a mop of short, lush dark-blonde hair and what could euphemistically be called a pugilist's face. Nick was so hairy his jock buddies nicknamed him "Wolfman." Let's just say that with his blunt nose, curly ears and caterpillar eyebrows, Nick Cipriano had never been considered a great beauty even though he was one of the most accomplished athlete's in the school and very popular. Didn't matter to me. He totally turned me on and I had to be careful not to stare too much. I tried talking with him a couple of times but I didn't really get close enough and I was too shy to walk right up to him.

My fantasy was always some variation on running into Nick in front of his house while his parents were away: helping him to load some furniture into a truck, helping to hoist him up to a window because he'd forgotten his keys, or coming by in a snow storm without a coat and needing shelter because my car broke down. And while sometimes in my fantasy something spilled on him and he had to remove his shirt and pants or other times he needed to take a shower for some reason, usually it was just our eyes that met after which he grabbed me and pressed his lips against mine. And after he'd kissed me for a long time, pushing me onto the floor with all his weight, he'd tell me that Betty Collins wouldn't suck his cock because she said it was too big and because he was uncut and wouldn't I please, please suck his cock for him. I would gladly of course and after we'd taken off the rest of our clothes I would imagine Nick reaching up to my shoulder to firmly push me down to my knees. He would gently grab a handful of my hair and pull my head back with one hand while with the other hand he would slowly guide his hardening cock into my mouth so I could feel the weight of it, get it wet with saliva and feel it lengthen and harden on my tongue.

Just then I opened my eyes, and saw two men standing about fifteen feet in front me. A strange kind of guttural sound leapt from my throat as I shoved my cock and balls back in my pants so fast it hurt and jumped off the boulder and onto my feet zipping up my coat. At the same time, the taller of the two men put his hands up in front of him saying, "Whoa there! Sorry, sorry, sorry. Didn't mean to scare you." Naturally scared and surprised, having thought I was alone, my impulse was to bolt. The top of my body jerked as it if I might run, but my feet wouldn't move.

"Gave you quite a jolt and I'm sorry about that, son." said the taller and older man now actually looking sorry, as he dropped his hands and shook his head. When he looked up at me I could see for the first time that he was handsome, with a slender face, heavy five o'clock shadow, thick hair, laugh lines, frown lines, smile lines, and all without being wrinkly. He was quite tall and probably only in his mid-fifties but to me at age seventeen, a man obviously a good deal older than my father was just plain-old old.

"Are you all right?" asked the younger man.

With my heart pounding and my throat dry, I was just able to speak, "Sure." I was a certified virgin who had gotten comfortable with his jack off routine, and though not brazen it certainly never occurred to me what it would feel like to be caught. It felt bad. I felt so guilty and so humiliated, but I was trying to stand my ground, to act like it didn't matter. My heavy breathing, shaking knees, still-hard cock, and what I can only imagine was a flushed and mortified face, belied any pretense of confidence or nonchalance I might have hoped for.

The younger man spoke again, "All guys beat off, you know. It's no big deal."

"I know that," I said sounding childish, but immediately wished I hadn't.

The younger man was younger in that he was probably thirty-five but he was still plenty older than me. He took off his winter cap and I could see that in addition to his full brown beard, well, there wasn't anything in addition, he was bald. On the heavy side, he looked strong and his eyes were piercing and brown. They reminded me of an animal's eyes. I wondered why the three of us were standing there and why none of us had walked away. Then I noticed that both men had bulges in their pants. The younger man was touching his.

The taller man took a step forward as he said, "Well it's all right now. We're all men here and you'll want to get back to what you were doing."

"Ya, right." I said softly, feeling silly and angry.

"Of course you will," he continued "you were real hot with your large hand on your throbbing horsecock there. You looked beautiful, a handsome young man like you with those big balls bouncing up and down. Just beautiful."

Now I was embarrassed in a different way. Beautiful? No one had ever called me that and it didn't sound right. It sounded peculiar, but it felt good. I'd never considered that I might have beauty of any kind.

"I'm sorry we got caught watching you," said the younger man. "You can go ahead and start stroking yourself again, and we can keep a look out for you."

I looked at their boots. The younger man wore black military boots, like a private would wear, and the older man had on brown hunter's boots. The brown boots stepped closer to me. I looked up and he stopped.

"I have a better idea," he said. "How would like to have your cock sucked? Has anybody ever given you a blowjob?" I knew what a blowjob was and I knew I wanted to give them and to get them. I had wanted to for years and I wanted one badly right then. I couldn't speak. "Has anyone done that for you, son? Given you a proper cock-sucking?"

I shook my head 'no,' very slowly.

The bearded man stepped forward and spoke, "Well, then you should let Charles suck you off. He's the..."

Charles shushed his friend, and stood looking at me. After perhaps a minute, an extremely long, loud minute, he said, "If you didn't want me to suck your cock you'd be way up the trail and out of sight by now." He put his hand on my shoulder and I flinched. "Now scoot yourself back up on that rock, son. Go ahead."

Putting my hands behind me up on the boulder I pushed and hoisted myself back up to the spot where I was sitting before. I saw Charles's hands reaching for the zipper on my winter coat. I flinched again, but didn't stop him from opening my zipper. I looked at him then and thought about his lips, the shadow of his stubble, his teeth, and I started to see how sexy he was. He then managed with great skill to extract my balls and hard cock. Of course his hands were terribly cold, but that didn't bother me. No one had ever handled my cock before and it felt strange and wonderful. He then undid my belt and the button on my jeans and grabbed either side up by my belt and started to pull. I resisted.

"Don't worry. It will feel better this way. I promise. Eric will keep a look out in case anyone comes by." I relented, rocking forward and back until he could slip the jeans out from under me and pull them down to my ankles. I was thinking he'd never get my boots off that way and I didn't want them taken off. It felt like he was stepping on my underwear so I leaned forward to see that he had stepped over my underwear and bunched up jeans and, widening his stance, was effectively binding my legs. I thought for sure he was going to take me in his mouth then. He was directly in front of my dick which was sticking straight up, about seven and a half inches then, and pulsing as precum trickled out.

The bearded guy Eric, then scrambled up the side of boulder until he was crouching right behind me. Just as I was starting to turn to see what he was doing, Charles reached out with a tongue like a German Shepherd and licked the head of my cock right around the piss slit. I gasped. Eric's hands were on my shoulders and moving down, down into my open coat and then his thick hands were moving across my t-shirt. I was still watching Charles to see if he would lick me again and he did, twice more, quickly around the head, but with strength in his tongue that was uncanny. Eric was massaging my chest as he pulled my t-shirt up over my head and, leaving my arms in the t-shirt sleeves, pulled my coat down.

Finally I found my voice. "I think it's too cold here…for this."

"It won't be too cold once you're all heated up, son. In the meantime, Eric, take off your coat for our friend to sit on." Eric took off his coat and folded it and tucked it under me. Charles's hot breath was on my cock. Then Eric got behind me again and pulled my t-shirt and coat all the way down to my wrists. I could feel his weight, his knees, on my coat and then his sweater and his beard against my back and neck. I couldn't move. I tried to move my arms and I couldn't. I could only move my legs in a little side-to-side motion. I had a picture in my mind of the three of us like that out in the woods alone and I realized, fully, for the first time, that there were two of them and only one of me. I panicked.

"Let me go, let me go!" I said.

Immediately I felt Eric stand up and start to pull my coat back up while Charles stepped back and started to pull my pants up.

"Wait," I said. They stopped. I didn't know what to say. I glanced up at Charles who seemed to be patiently waiting for me to make up my mind. I realized that they had no intention of hurting me. I had wanted for so long to have sex with a guy. This scenario wasn't anything I had in mind, but I wasn't going to lose my chance. My dick was standing up as hard as ever. It seemed like it was hard during my entire adolescence, but now it was so hard it hurt a little.

"You can only stay here if you want to, son." Charles said. "No one will make you."

My breath was steaming as I sat there. My mind was blank. Then I thought of Charles sucking me. "Okay," I said. "I want to stay."

Within a moment my t-shirt and coat were back down to my wrists with Eric against my back, and my pants were down to my ankles with Charles standing between and spreading my legs, his hot breath exhaling onto my balls.

By age seventeen I was just over six feet tall and, though I hadn't filled out completely and didn't participate in sports, you wouldn't have called me scrawny or thin. I weighed about 175 pounds. Except for the wavy dark hair on my head, the big black bushes of hair under my arms, a little hair around my asshole, and my big bush of pubic hair that some of the black guys in gym class called my "Afro," I wasn't at all hairy — that would come later. And there I was, naked and nearly hairless from head to ankles, arms stretched behind me, dick sticking straight up, ready.

Charles leaned in a little — his face was almost perfectly positioned in front of my crotch — and with his muscular tongue he began to lick from the base to the head of my cock on the sides and the underside. My cock would bounce a little in response. He was methodical and firm. Eric started to run the fingertips of his meaty hands lightly over my chest and I started to notice that as he passed over my nipples they seemed to grow and he would stub a finger on them the way you might stub your toe on a little stone if your were dragging your foot. Every time Eric began to repeat a pattern with his fingers over my chest and stomach he would change it and move his hands in a different way or at a different speed. It felt good but it also felt ticklish and accentuated the coldness of the air. Charles coated my whole cock, front and back, top to bottom with mixture of saliva and precum. It seemed that the more fluid he made the less pressure he used so that he was kind of tickling of my cock the way Eric was tickling my chest and stomach.

Eric placed a hand on my forehead, guiding my head back. "Relax," he said, "just relax." He was right, I wasn't relaxed, but I was certainly turned on. I tried to relax and I let my head kind of loll back, looking up occasionally when Charles was doing yet another amazing thing with his mouth. I could feel the first time he touched his lips to the head of my cock and then it felt liked someone was putting a silk condom on me, then taking it off, then putting it on, all the way up and off, all the way down to my bush and my balls, increasing speed, just a little, each time. It wasn't till later of course that I wondered about how Charles had learned to do what he did so skillfully. During that hour I spent with Charles and Eric on the boulder I wanted to learn what they were doing and I couldn't help watching and feeling, but mostly I just fell deeper and deeper under a spell that I have never experienced since.

While Eric gently tweaked my nipples and licked my ears, Charles lifted my legs, and gave my balls, cock, and thighs a thorough tongue bath that left me breathing heavily and wishing he would just plunge his mouth down on my cock and suck and suck until I came. Instead, he raised my legs even higher and did something that surprised and thrilled me. Charles began flicking his enormous tongue around my asshole. I wondered what it smelled like but I knew it must have been okay since Charles used his tongue more and more forcefully until he had me very wet. The feeling was heavenly. Then he pushed his tongue right against my sphincter and it dawned on me that he was trying to get into my asshole! They both must have felt my fear because Charles started stroking my legs while Eric guided my head back again and, holding my head while resting my upper body on his lap — I could feel his cock throbbing against my back — he sweetly began to kiss me. I kissed back. I had never kissed anyone before and I closed my eyes and I was kissing Nick Cipriano, the same full lips, the same sexy face I had dreamed about. The practice I had kissing in my masturbation fantasies must have paid off because I made out with Eric for a long time while Charles fucked my ass with his mighty tongue. Charles's tongue fucking was probably the equivalent of getting finger fucked by one short thick finger. But at that time it all was new and every little thrust from

Charles, every penetration sent surges of pleasure from my feet up through my nipples that were being lightly tugged by Eric as he kissed me.

I heard myself moaning. It jarred me a little when it got loud enough that I noticed, so I stopped for a moment to listen. Beside the soft sounds of licking and kissing I could only hear the wind in the trees and the shuddering of the leaves in their branches. Charles's continued massaging and poking of my sphincter brought me back to the moment. I let go again, and let the sounds come out of me as they would. Eric helped me to sit back up and he removed my coat entirely, but kept my t-shirt over my head and used it to secure my hands behind my head then laid me back down. With my hands wrapped in my t-shirt, supporting my head, Eric was able to lick and bite my armpits, and he did. At the same time Charles licked his way back up to my cock and began to give me the blow job, or "proper cocksucking" as he put it, that he originally offered.

In some ways it is hard to describe the blowjob I got from Charles. I know it started with a slow mild suction as his lips moved gradually from the base of my cock to the head and back again — the head of my cock snug and deep in his throat when his lips were at the base — and a slow curling and licking of his tongue on the way up and the way down. The more he sucked, the deeper I fell into a kind of bliss that made me aware of every physical sensation — the tongues, the lips, the teeth, the stubble, the hands, the cold boulder, the cold wind, the creaking trees — and at the same time made feel removed, drifting, floating above the physical to a place where I was intoxicated, and I was getting higher and higher. I did notice that Charles never picked up speed and he never sucked me hard. Something about the steadiness of his rhythm and his pressure kept me suspended in the feelings of bliss but also didn't allow me to come.

By now Eric was eating my hairy armpits. He bit and chewed and rubbed his whole face around under each arm. At first it seemed a little rough — it was another pleasure I had never known or considered — but the more steadily Charles continued sucking me the more I wanted Eric to lick, bite and chew harder in my pits.

I moaned even louder and I wanted to come. For a moment Charles he increased the speed and intensity of his sucking but then he moved down and starting licking and sucking my balls. It was sweet but it was also torture. Once in a while Charles would run his tongue up the length of my cock or slurp around the head and I would start to feel like I was going to come, mercifully I was going to release my load, but then he would go back to my balls. He kept this up until I thought I couldn't stand it anymore. My cock stood straight up. It was enormous. I never thought my cock was all that big but it had swollen and grown and was so hard that it bobbed a little. Charles's head started to move up from my balls to my cock again I put my head back down. "Here we go," I thought. Charles licked and slurped and sucked and I was so close to coming but I just wouldn't come! It was like a prolonged orgasm but it was not an actual orgasm. The feelings of pleasure were making me higher and higher. I felt kind of numb. Of course I had recognized that particular moment right before orgasm, that remarkable moment when you know you're going to shoot. But now I was having that sensation dozens of times without actually coming, and I didn't think I could endure it anymore. I could feel tears running down my cheeks, they started to come faster until I could feel them on my neck and in my ears. I spoke softly at first, then a little louder. "Please. Please. Please let me come," I said. I didn't think they could hear me so as I cried, I called out "Please. Please. Please. Oh, please." Charles stopped and looked at me from behind my cock.

"Let go." he said. "Just let go, son."

I wasn't sure exactly what he meant but I was desperate. So, as the tears continued running, I said it to myself, "Just let go. Just let go." It happened. I'm not sure how. Maybe I stopped trying to come. I let go. And as my body gave way even more, Eric held up my head so I could watch Charles make one lick from the base to the head of my cock creating a sensation that felt as if I had been prodded by electricity as I watched a heavy load of my cum shoot up in the air, distributed by my pulsing cock over my chest and Charles's hair. I moaned. He licked again, I shot again, My head dropped back in ecstasy and the next thing I knew Charles had swallowed my cock whole and Eric had covered my mouth with his. I could taste the sweat from under my arms on Eric's tongue as Charles sucked three more electric shots of cum out of my cock, and then sucked and nibbled me while my cock pulsed for the next several minutes or so spitting out smaller and smaller amounts of cum, all of which Charles swallowed, humming with pleasure.

My body was still convulsing after I came. Eric and Charles just kept licking, kissing and sucking me until it seemed like they were licking all over my body. It felt like they were cleaning me. I felt they were loving me.

After a minute or two I was being kissed again. It was Charles now. I didn't know what a cock tasted like, but I suspected that the musky, delicious taste I was tasting in Charles's mouth was the taste of my cock and sperm. Then he licked some of the tears that were dried on my neck.

Eric was sucking my gradually softening cock, cleaning it and massaging it. Soon I began to feel the cold and it was making me shiver. Eric and Charles helped me up and helped me to clean up and get dressed. They both lit cigarettes and offered me one that I took. We stood silently smoking. Charles asked me which way I was walking home. I pointed. They were going the other way.

"Are you all right?" asked Charles.

"Oh, yes, of course." I said. "Thank you. Thank you guys, for ..." I couldn't finish. There were so many things I wanted to say — questions I wanted to ask — but it was all so sudden and they were leaving.

"Take care of yourself," Charles said as they turned and walked away.

After they'd gotten twenty feet or so Eric turned and shouted, "And, be good!"

"I will." I said, not sure that they had heard me.

So what has happened in the thirty-two years since that chilly afternoon? Well, among other things, I did fill out eventually, got very big all over, and grew a pelt of hair on my chest, belly, legs, arms and back. I met a lot of men and fucked many of them. Due in part I think to my size and look, and in part to my inclinations, I became a friendly, perhaps garden variety, top bear, and a good one. Still, every once in a while an opportunity arises when I can utilize my skills as a cocksucker. One such opportunity came up recently with a fifty-year-old stud who was clearly in need of a proper cock-sucking. Well, I know I'm pretty good, but I knew I was still very, very good when after forty minutes or so I heard Nick Cipriano whisper, as he tightened his grasp on my hair, "Please ... please! Oh, please, let me come. *Please* ... !"

Kelvin Williams *is a freelance writer of travel and erotica. Williams also works as a carpenter and makes furniture in Milwaukee where he lives with his Airedale Terrier, Angus. His sex stories have been published in* Cruise Lines, Travelrotica 2, *and* My First Time 4, *and* How the West Was Done.

Miners

Wayne Mansfield

Duke pushed the door to the small metal cabin open and saw his new roommate sitting on the bed looking at some papers.

"Hey, you must be Josh," he said pulling the door shut with one hand and holding out the other.

Josh looked up at the burly man and stood up. They shook hands.

"That's right," said Josh. "Just got in late this afternoon. I didn't realize how far out this mine site was. I worked in Kalgoorlie for a while but this is out in the middle of nowhere."

Duke smiled to himself as he took his jacket off. "Yeah, it's a bit of a shock at first but just wait till you start doing the twelve hour shifts. You won't care where you are. You'll climb into that bed there and never want to leave. "

He laughed a great booming laugh.

"I'd stay up and have a drink with you, mate, but I want to get some sleep. You'll understand once you've done a few shifts. Which team you on?"

"C Team," Josh replied. "We don't start till tomorrow afternoon."

Duke began to unbutton his shirt. "I'm A Team we start in the morning. I guess that's why they put us in together. You'll be getting in just as I'm heading out."

Duke pulled his plaid shirt off to reveal a barrel chest covered in a thick mat of fur. Two large nipples sat atop the solid mounds of his pectoral muscles, sticking out from the fur like teats. His arms were massive, the forearms thickly haired while a tattoo of a mermaid rippled on the skin over his left bicep.

"You gonna grab some sleep, too?" Duke asked his hands busy at his belt buckle. "Or you gonna head over to the mess hall?"

Josh shrugged his broad shoulders. "Might as well hit the sack," he replied. "I guess I'm a bit tired after the flight up."

He unbuttoned his shirt while Duke pulled his work boots off. Soon the room was filled with the smell of sweaty feet. The boots were left where they dropped and the socks tossed into a corner.

"Sorry about the smell, mate," said Duke. "Occupational hazard."

They shared a laugh as they undressed. Josh pulled his boots and socks off while Duke slipped his Levis and jocks down. When the giant man leaned down to pull his jeans off Josh found himself unable to take his eyes off the man's thick, solid thighs and lightly-haired butt cheeks, which had parted a little so that Josh could see the nest of dark hair that lined his room mate's asscrack. He felt himself getting hard and a flood of panic swept through his body. He fumbled at his own belt buckle, his jeans falling to the linoleum just as Duke turned around.

"I might snore, mate, so I'm gonna apologize in advance," he said with a smile, his teeth brilliantly white against the deep red of his lips and the dark brown of his thick moustache and goatee. Then he looked down. "Fuck, mate. What's that?!"

Josh didn't have to look. His eight-incher was poking out at right angles from his thick bush of black pubic hair. There was nothing he could do about it now. And when he glanced down at Duke's slab of man meat hanging down like an extra limb over a set of the biggest balls he'd ever seen, he felt it twitch.

Duke stepped toward Josh and grabbed his cock. Without speaking he started tugging it, his eyes glued to Josh's.

Josh could feel Duke's uncut nine-incher growing against the muscles of his thigh. He felt Duke pushing it against him, grinding it against the hairy skin, and then the tickle of a dribble of precum.

"Oh mate, that feels —" Josh began, but Duke pressed his lips against his mouth and cut him short. Duke kissed him with a pent up passion. It had been a while since Josh had had any man-to-man contact but it had been even longer for Duke. Up on the mine site Duke was respected, not just because of his size but because he was considered to be man's man. There was no messing around with him. He worked hard and expected everyone else to pull his weight. He had been careful not to jeopardize that image. But when he had seen Josh's solid body, his hairy six-pack and huge, hard cock he knew he could make a move without fear of retribution.

Duke's tongue probed Josh's mouth, their tongues licking, sucking and tasting each other. Their mouths moved hungrily against each other. Duke licked the hair above Josh's lip then ran his flattened tongue down over his lips, settling on Josh's bristled chin. He bit on it gently, scraping the bristles with his teeth before giving it a suck.

He heard Josh moan as his expert mouth explored the skin of his neck, which was rough, unshaved, and tasted salty. He maneuvered his tongue down over one hairy pectoral muscle, taking Josh's nipple in his mouth and biting it just enough to make Josh yelp. He smiled as he continued to suck on the small nub of flesh, taking it between his teeth and flicking it with the firm tip of his tongue.

Josh felt electric. The man's mouth on his hairy tit would have been enough to make him blow his load over the dirty linoleum of the floor right then and there, but it was too soon for that. Even though he could feel his hairy balls tightening he wasn't going to shoot yet. He put his hands on Duke's head and pushed the man down to where his cock was straining, eager to be sucked. And when he felt Duke's warm, wet mouth envelope it, he exhaled deeply.

Duke squatted in front of his new roommate; his puckered hole exposed to the night air creeping in through the bottom of the door, and slid his mouth onto the stiff pole in front of his face. He easily swallowed all eight inches down the back of his throat, leaving it there, enjoying the feeling of being full of cock, before the need for oxygen forced him to come up for air. Again he swallowed the cock, running his tongue over the veins that snaked their way along the shaft. As he came back up the cock he ran his tongue over the swollen, fleshy cock-head, sucking on it, tonguing the piss slit and detecting the taste of stale piss. As his mouth continued to slide up and down the meaty shaft he could hear Josh groaning. His new roommate's hands were heavy on his head, pulling him deeper and deeper onto his cock until he thought he might choke on it.

Then Duke took his mouth off Josh's cock and spun him around. With one powerful hand he pushed Josh forward so that he half-fell against the metal frame of the single bed. He grabbed a chunk of arse flesh with each hand and pulled Josh's arse cheeks roughly apart to reveal a dark pink pucker surrounded by a thick ring of black hair. He put his nose to it and breathed in the musty, earthy scent of man cunt. His cock twitched between his legs demanding attention so it was with pleasure he grabbed it and started pumping it as he inhaled the stink of Josh's sweaty hole.

Josh wrapped his hand around his own swollen staff and started tugging it. He could hear Duke sniffing around his hole and the idea that someone was getting off on the smell of his unwashed chute made his cock so hard he thought it would split in two. And he actually gasped when he felt Duke's firm, wet tongue probing the puckered flesh of his asshole, pressing against the muscle, eager to get inside. Instinctively he arched his back and pushed his tight fuck-hole further into Duke's face, his wrinkled pucker tightening whenever the hair of Duke's goatee rubbed against it, scratching and tickling.

Duke pulled Josh's meat cushions apart and pushed his face hard against the pucker. His tongue prodded and probed until it pushed through the muscle. He felt the smooth, slimy tissue of Josh's anal lining on his tongue and started licking and nibbling at the flesh like a hungry animal, rubbing his face over it to coat himself in Josh's man smell.

Between his legs his cock was as hard as steel and well coated in precum. The veins of his cock glistened under the electric light and the massive helmet, which capped the thick shaft, throbbed as liters of precum spilled out onto the floor. There was a tightening there too. His heavy balls had begun to draw up into his body.

In silence he stood up.

Josh continued to stroke his cock. His pucker was glowing from the combined action of Duke's tongue and face fur against it. Strings of his own manmade lube were dribbling out of his piss slit, stretching toward the blankets on the bed before snapping to join an ever-growing dark wet patch in the grey wool of his own bedding.

Duke spat into the small pool of precum he had collected in his hand and then wiped the lot over Josh's hole.

"Be careful, mate," Josh said. He knew what was about to happen and he wanted it more than anything at that moment, but he had also seen the size of Duke's mammoth organ. He'd never taken anything that size before.

Duke didn't reply. Instead he pushed the slippery head of his cock against Josh's hole. At first there was some resistance. He had been expecting that. It was a natural reaction to something so large trying to enter something so tight, so small. He massaged his cock-head against the sphincter, rubbing it in small circles and pressing ever harder until finally he pushed the head through. He paused a moment to let Josh get accustomed to it then he slowly slid the whole nine inches inside, each small thrust producing a sharp inhalation from Josh.

Josh gritted his teeth. His eyes were shut tight as he concentrated on keeping his ass muscles relaxed and mouth closed. He was a man of thirty-two, not some boy. His ass would soon get used to it. He just had to give it time. His hand started tugging a little faster on his cock. That helped a bit.

Duke eased his way in taking as much care as he could. It was difficult to hold back. Now that most of cock was inside Josh all he wanted to do was start pounding that sweet hole. Instead he thrust gently. His hips barely moving at first but as he felt the anal muscles relax around his pole he picked up the pace. He gripped Josh's hips with his big paws and brought the man's ass back to meet his thrusts. Faster and faster he punched his cock into the warmth of Josh's fuck-tunnel until he realized that he was giving it the pounding he'd wanted to give it ever since he realized Josh liked cock.

Josh kept his eyes closed but his jaws were no longer clenched together. In fact it felt good to feel so full of cock. Every now and again when Duke got a bit carried away there was a flash of pain. But it felt good to have this he-man inside him, using his ass for his pleasure, his massive hands pulling him roughly onto his cock. Splashes of the man's sweat hit his back and his grunts filled his ears. Duke's full balls slapped against the hairy skin between his legs, sticking slightly with each thrust before peeling away to slap against Duke's groin. He could smell sex in the air — sweat, salt, arse juice, and precum. He breathed it in, concentrated on those things rather than any discomfort in his ass.

Duke looked down at his cock as it slid in and out of Josh's arse. He could see the skin of his room mate's asshole stretched taut over his thick prick, the pink skin almost white as it was pulled out on his cock. His fat pole was glistening with a combination of arse juice and his own precum, and he noticed the hair of Josh's ass crack was damp and stuck down to the pale white flesh too. He spat onto his cock and watched the bubbles of his saliva disappear into Josh's man-cunt.

Now that Josh's ass was his he began ramming his cock deeper and deeper in. His whole body was coated in sweat and the hair on his chest was laying in black clumps against the tight, tanned skin of his torso. He could feel his balls tightening and a familiar feeling growing in his groin. It wouldn't be long now.

Josh's nuts were no more than two hairy lumps on his groin. His cock-head had swollen and was now a shiny pink mushroom ready to explode. Behind him Duke was ploughing his hole, his massive cock massaging his rock hard prostate. It was impossible to resist.

"I have to shoot, mate. I have to fuckin' shoot," he moaned.

Duke did not reply.

Josh's hand flew up and down the length of his cock, firm and fast. In seconds he was rewarded with a geyser of pearly white mancream, which shot across the grey blanket beneath. Jet after jet rocketed out, one squirt hitting the wall on the other side of the bed. He shuddered as the last few drops of cock juice spotted the already cum-stained bedding.

As Josh blew his wad his ass muscles tightened, clamping down on Duke's cock and not even a man like him could resist the warm, wet pressure on his engorged cock. He pulled his cock out of Josh's cunt with a popping sound and spun the man around. Josh lost his balance and ended up sitting on the edge of the bed, his dripping cock still semi-hard. That was cool with Duke. He couldn't have planned it better. His load hit Josh squarely in the face. He jerked his massive cock off as a great tsunami of jizz splattered across the whiskered skin of Josh's face. The sight of his ball-cream running down the tanned skin through the three-day growth and then dripping off onto his hairy chest seemed to extend the life of Duke's orgasm. More and more ball-juice flew out until Josh was drenched in the stuff.

"Open up," Duke growled.

Josh did as he was told, letting the massive cock invade his mouth. The back of his throat immediately felt the last of Duke's cum hit it and he swallowed the sweet paste down.

"Suck it," said Duke as he placed a hand on the back of Josh's head.

Josh closed his mouth around the thick cock and slid his lips up and down its length. The smell of his arse was strong on it and so was the taste of cum. He couldn't stop thinking about how it had felt inside him. Then he realized that his softening cock had started to grow again.

"You're a fuckin' machine," Duke said as he noticed Josh's cock stiffening.

Then Josh felt something salty hit the back of his throat. He took his mouth off Duke's cock and felt his chin and neck get sprayed with Duke's piss. He looked up at Duke who was smiling back at him, one of his hands coming down to grasp his pissing cock.

"This means you're mine, buddy. I'm marking you so no other bastard up here can have you. I've waited too long to meet a guy I can, er, pass the time with. Deal?"

Josh nodded. "Okay, mate."

Duke directed the stream of piss over Josh's chest so that it splashed against first one nipple and then another, before he lowered his aim and splashed some over his rock-hard cock.

"I see you're liking this," Duke grinned.

"Fuck yeah," Josh relied. "Never done this before. Feels hot."

With one hand on his cock Josh brought the other one up to his furry chest and ran it over the piss-soaked hair.

Duke lifted his cock and resprayed the man's chest, dousing it with man piss so that soon Josh was dripping. Then he raised it even higher, letting the golden arc hit Josh on the chin. Instinctively Josh opened his mouth and let the last of Duke's piss squirt into his mouth and run down the back of his throat. He swallowed hard, keeping up with the volume of piss that was landing in his mouth. Then as the stream dwindled to a few dribbles, Duke leaned down and kissed him on the lips, his own mouth sucking up the remnants of piss that had beaded on the skin around his mouth.

"Next time that load will go up your ass, buddy," he said.

"Which load?" Josh asked, feeling foolish.

"Both of them," Duke replied as he clamped his lips down on Josh's.

Both pairs of lips were salty and their kisses were just as feverish as they had been when they first started.

Duke pushed Josh back so that he had to scoot across the bed until his back was against the wall then he climbed onto the bed and positioned his hole over Josh's hard cock.

"I don't know if I can go again, Duke."

Duke sat down on Josh's cock, his eyes closing as the eight-inch pole disappeared inside him.

"Don't matter," Duke replied as his lips found Josh's. "I just want to feel you inside me."

Duke was on his knees. He used them to lever himself up and down on Josh's cock. Josh, who was sitting with his legs straight out in front of him was powerless to move. They were both beefy men, but Duke was larger and had him pinned to the bed. He wrapped his arms around Duke's broad shoulders and pressed his lips to Duke's. Their tongues roamed over each other, slipping and entwining as Duke rocked himself against the stiffness of the cock that was buried in his hairy cunt.

Josh pulled Duke closer to him so that their hairy chests touched, pec to pec, nipple to nipple. Their kisses were hungry as both of them began to feel that a second load was possible. Minutes passed by unnoticed as both men lost themselves in the passion of their piss-flavored kisses.

Then without warning, Duke reached in front of him and grabbed his cock. There was no smooth beginning. His hand started jerking the massive piece of meat like a piston and he began rocking frantically on the eight inches he was impaled on. The action of his ass on Josh's hips was making the walls of the portable unit rock. For the moment Duke had forgotten years of past discretion. He was lost in the wave of sensation caused by a second load brewing in his balls.

"I'm gonna come again," Josh mumbled into his mouth.

"Me too, buddy. You gonna blow now?"

"Yeah," Josh replied, his breathy answer being inhaled by Duke. "Right fuckin' now!"

They grunted into each other's mouth as Josh blew a load up inside Duke's tight fuckhole while Duke coated the fur on Josh's chest with thick man-glue. Even though they had blown only minutes before, Duke's second load was considerable, the result of weeks of pent-up sexual energy and the fact that Josh was so hot. A real man. Not some city boy who didn't know what to do with the equipment God had given him.

Duke scooped some of his cum up with a couple of fingers and fed it to Josh, who sucked them clean.

"Well that was fuckin' amazing," Duke said as he climbed off Josh's cock, a thick stream of cum escaping from his hairy pucker and running down the inside of his thigh as he stood up. "Now we'd better get this mess cleaned up. You can sleep with me tonight," he said nodding toward the small single bed, "and then in the morning you can do the laundry. But we'd better wipe this piss up or else it'll start stinking when the heat of the sun gets to it tomorrow."

Josh smiled. A bit of cleaning up was a small price to pay for such a hot fuck. And he got to sleep with the man, although he didn't know how much sleep they'd get, shift or no shift.

__Wayne Mansfield__ was born and raised in rural Western Australia. He now lives and works in Perth, and is a nudist and regular beachgoer. He teaches English to overseas students and is a school counselor. His writing has appeared in many collections of gay erotica and online collections.

Desmond

Jared Bascomb

Forty of us gathered at the incident command post at the Rancho La Fonda Community Center at 8:00am. The firestorm that had swept through three days earlier was still raging to the north and east, but the community itself was out of danger. But before the evacuated residents could return to their homes — if they had homes to return to — the fire-ravaged neighborhoods had to be inspected for safety and habitability.

That was my job. Three inspectors would be taken by patrol car to an assigned area within the cordoned-off neighborhood. Once there, we would split up and perform our house-by-house evaluations on foot and make our way back to the post. Meanwhile, the police officer would cruise the area by car, patrolling for looters, gawkers, and other trespassers.

When the briefing was over, we all made our way to the parking lot where a fleet of patrol cars waited for us. I and the other two members of Team 17B were assigned to a car driven by an officer whose brass nametag identified him as P Desmond.

A guy named Patrick Desmond had been the star linebacker on my high school's football team, and I wondered if this cop could be him. The two Desmonds had the same rust-colored hair and green eyes, and Officer Desmond was ex-linebacker large, with the additional poundage that comes with aging 25 years. He was so big that I was amazed that a guy his size could fit into the Crown Vic. At six-two, I had to scrunch up to get into the front passenger seat, and he had about three inches and a good fifty pounds on me.

Before I could ask him about our possible connection, Officer Desmond went into a spiel about our responsibilities in the fire zone. When he finished his speech, an inspector in the back seat said, "Must be pretty rough on you guys."

Desmond ran his fingers through his hair and down over his face, the heavy beard stubble rasping against the palm of his hand. "Shit, yeah. I'm on my fourth day of double-shifts. I've been in this car for eleven hours already today. I get done with you guys and I'm off-duty. So make it fast, okay?"

He braked at the corner of Via de las Piedras and Paseo Valle Vista. "This is your stop, buddy." He pointed to my walkie-talkie. "You need any help, just radio me on channel 17," and drove away with the other two inspectors.

I walked the deserted streets, checking for structural damage, availability of electrical power, and damage to roads and other infrastructure, all the while considering whether Officer Desmond was my ex-schoolmate.

He was certainly big enough to be "Desmond the Destroyer," the linebacker who mowed down his opponents on the football field. His hairy forearms suggested that he might be the adult version of the high-schooler who'd been called "King Kong" and "Ape-Man" because of his premature and excessive hirsuteness.

And then there was the truly crude nickname Patrick Desmond had been given because of the size of his penis. I'd never seen it, so I had no idea if the stories were true or not, but every time I'd jacked off I'd fantasized about servicing the hairy upperclassman's equipment.

My reminiscences of adolescent jack-off sessions ended abruptly when I arrived at the final street on my route. Most of the homeowners in my sector had lucked out: their houses were intact, and the only evidence that there had been a major conflagration nearby was the layer of ash and the still-strong smell of smoke.

The residents of Calle del Cielo were not so fortunate. All that remained was the long road itself, climbing a hill that was a wasteland of rubble and ruin. Every house was gone as far as the eye could see. But my eye couldn't see the cul-de-sac at the summit. It would have been an easy matter to just write off the entire street, but duty required that I make the trek to the top in the mid-day sun to document the destruction. I took a swig of bottled water, opened my shirt to let in some air, and started up the steep incline.

I was partway up the hill when the police car stopped beside me. "Want a lift?"

Officer Desmond didn't have to ask twice. He drove slowly while I verified the parcel numbers of the ruins against my list. Sometimes it was hard to tell where one property ended and another began. When we passed one lot, I couldn't help chuckling.

"What's so funny?"

"The whole place is in ashes. Everything's burned down — except the backyard barbecue grill."

Desmond shook his head. "Jeezus, you've got a warped sense of humor. Should've been a cop."

He continued up the hill. When we reached the summit, he slammed on the brakes. "Holy fucking shit! Can you believe that?"

The entire cul-de-sac had been destroyed by the fire, every home reduced to rubble. Except one. At the very end of the street, a single house stood intact. Its stucco walls were blackened and its windows were blown out from the inferno, but it stood there as a testimony to the vagaries of fire.

I recorded the lot numbers of the burnt-out residences as I walked toward the lone remaining structure. A singed wooden gate still protected the back yard even though the fence it was attached to was charcoal. A layer of ash covered the back yard's burnt lawn, concrete patio/deck, and swimming pool.

Officer Desmond and I stood in the blazing sun, gazing out at the charred valley below. What had been a million-dollar view was gone for at least twenty years.

He finally broke the silence. "Fuckin' hot man."

"Yeah. It's a real scorcher, all right."

"You didn't hear me right. I said, 'Fuckin' hot *man*'."

The cop grabbed my head and planted his mouth on mine so hard he damn near broke my teeth. His hungry moan eliminated any resistance on my part and I let his tongue slide inside. While we sucked and gnawed on each other, Desmond pawed my hardening cock.

"God-damn, that's fuckin' nice meat."

In one move he dropped to a squat, tore open my pants, and yanked down my briefs. Freed from the tight confinement of my jockeys, my dick sprang out and smacked the cop's beard-stubbled face. Almost immediately his lips were in my short and curlies, his moans muffled by the meat in his mouth and my cry of "Oh jeezus!"

His freckled cheeks bulged as my cock swelled in appreciation until it was knocking at the entry to his gullet. This was the point where most guys turned back. And so did my man in blue. He wrapped his large paws one above the other on my shaft and lapped at the two inches of meat and the bulbous head that extended beyond his fists.

"Jeezus fuck. That's a huge fuckin' cock. I'm gonna take it all, god-damnit."

He pulled my balls until my dick was aimed downward, then opened wide and engulfed my shaft to its root, his face in my pubes again. But this time I was *hard*. Very few guys can swallow me, and no one had ever taken me so deep so quickly. It was like Desmond's throat had been specially designed to take my cock. The head was lodged somewhere deep inside a throat that squeezed and milked it for what seemed like an eternity while his tongue tap-danced along my shaft and his lips gnawed at my pubes.

"Oh fuck!" I gasped as my nuts struggled to escape his grasp and pull upward, desperate to unload.

The cop pulled off and gazed up at me, strings of spit hanging between his face and my crotch. "Yeah, fuck my face, man. Hard as you want. Hard as you can. Make me take it."

He slurped my cockhead back into his greedy mouth and down his throat, and put my hands on his head. I grabbed his red hair tight. He looked up at me and whimpered his need.

I pulled all the way back and slammed my cock back into him so hard I thought I'd broken his nose. Desmond gagged, but grunt-moaned his appreciation. So I let him have it.

And by gawd if the fucker didn't take it. Spit sprayed as I pummeled his mouth, and more spit dripped down his chin. His throat was both accommodating and clenching with a suction that just wouldn't quit. Whenever I pulled back, it was an effort to extract myself from his vacuuming throat, like he was fighting me for possession of my own cock.

I watched my thick shaft slide between his pursed lips. I was fucking face harder than I fuck ass, and gawd, was it beautiful. But when my gaze shifted below that accommodating mouth to the dark blue police uniform …

"Oh jeezus gawd! I'm gonna cum!"

Desmond pulled off and double-fisted my cock. "Hose me. Sperm my face."

My first cumshot was a thick streak from his forehead to his jaw, barely missing his begging eyes. "Fuck yeah!" The pig aimed my erupting cock upward, and jacked it harder and licked my balls as my jism geysered out and splattered all over his face.

When I had no more goo to give, the cop stood up. It took three swipes of his big hand to transfer my jism from his freckled face to his mouth. "Good stuff," he said as he licked his palm clean.

This was my chance. If the man before me really was "Desmond the Destroyer," I would finally be servicing the dick I'd yearned for. If he wasn't my Desmond, he was still a cop. And I'd always wanted to suck off a uniformed cop. Either way, I was a winner.

He seized my wrist before I could reach his zipper. "Look, buddy, I'll be up front and honest with you. What I really need is to get fucked good and hard by that huge fuckin' dick of yours."

"Let me suck you first."

"No. Just fuck me. It takes a big man to hit my button, and it looks like you're a guy who can do that."

I got a real nice show as Officer Desmond removed his equipment belt and stripped off his uniform down to his boxers. His once-firm pecs were sagging and there was a roll of fat around his waist, but he was still solid. His tattoos — a dragon on his right shoulder, a bulldog on his left bicep — were almost obscured by red hair as thick and dense and curly as wool.

He turned and walked toward the swimming pool. His back was as hairy as his front, a great mass of dense red curls. He yanked down his boxers and kicked them aside, but he didn't remove the jockstrap beneath. He grasped the pool ladder's heat-warped handrails, bent over, and thrust his furry ass out. He looked over his hairy shoulder and demanded, "C'mon, man. Fuck me."

He spread his cheeks. A strong odor of stale sweat and man-scent blasted out, the product of those long hours driving around in a patrol car.

"Give it to me good, man. I need cock up my butt real bad."

But I had my own needs, and his ass-odor was intoxicating. So instead of fucking him, I squatted and shoved my face into that stinky crevasse. I lapped at the sweat-salty hair, excavating through the tasty fur to find the treasure buried deep within. Desmond hissed with pleasure as I scarfed away until his rosebud was revealed: a pulsing purple knot that had seen more than its share of action and definitely wanted more.

I slid between his legs, grabbed his thighs, and pulled the big bastard down until he was hovering above my face. Desmond pooched his ass-pucker open wider and I sucked and chewed on the knot of muscle that presented itself so willingly. I pulled his hairy cheeks wide open and dined out on high-grade cop-cunt, reveling in his sweat and hair and man-musk.

The cop rode my face the way a cowboy rides a Brahma bull. He held onto the railing while he bucked and thrashed and demanded that I work his butthole harder. I gnawed and chewed and sucked on that hard knot of muscle until it opened wide enough for me to get two fingers from each hand inside and still have room for my tongue to go drilling for more ass-juice. The cop's tasty ass was fuckin' roomy, but I wondered if it was roomy enough to take my meat.

"Goddammit, I'm gonna get fucked!"

Desmond hoisted himself off my ravenous mouth, shifted his spit-drippy butt directly above my upward-aimed cock and dropped onto it, his entire weight crashing into my crotch.

"Oh jeezus fuck *yeah*!" he bellowed into the burnt-out valley.

His body was extended gargoyle-like over the ash-covered pool. Anchored by my cock and his grip on the ladder, he swung himself back and forth, his ass-channel sliding along the length of my dick, fucking himself while he alternately cursed and blessed what my meat was doing to his insides. His swaying body threatened to pull us both into the pool, so I clutched the railing instead of running my fingers through the sweaty red hair on his back.

"Oh jeezus *yes*!" Desmond howled as liquid splashed into the pool.

A flood of urine spurted through the mesh of his jockpouch into the ash-covered water. He ground his beefy ass around my embedded organ, coaxing even more piss out of his bladder.

When his stream became a dribble he grunted, "Goddamn! Now we can really fuck!"

Without breaking contact, he pivoted to face me. The cop used the fire-warped pool ladder to provide leverage for shoving himself onto my cock, whimpering as it went deeper into his accommodating ass and moaning whenever he bottomed out.

Desmond's butt was the eighth wonder of the world. He tightened his sphincter and kept it tight as he rose until just my cockhead was inside. Then he loosened up and plunged all the way back down, grabbed hold again, and hauled himself back up, using his ass to milk the cum out of my cock.

I was in cop-fucking heaven. So much so that we were several minutes into the fuck before I noticed the size of the bulge in his piss-soaked jockpouch. He was my Desmond, all right. No doubt about it. The rumors about his dick were true. And I was more determined than ever to get that thing inside me.

Sweat dripped from his face and streamed off his body, but Desmond showed no signs of ending his plunging and sucking and grinding. "Oh fuck, I need that cock deep inside me."

"Yeah, you're taking me real deep, man."

"Not deep enough. Not hard enough. I need *more* of that big fuckin' cock."

Desmond stood and hauled me to my feet and resumed his original position: bent over, his thick arms on the pool ladder, hairy ass thrust out.

"Now really goddamn *fuck* me. Plow me good and hard."

I spread his fleshy buttcheeks. His hole was puffy, surrounded by wet hair, but wide open and pulsing and dripping. And demanding more. I put my cockhead against that inviting entrance and teased it. "You really want it?"

"Goddamn *yes*! Gimme everything you got! God, I need it so bad!"

I sank my meat balls-deep into his well-fucked channel and ground my pubes against the tender flesh. Other men had begged for mercy when I'd done that, but not my man in blue. *He* begged for more.

And I gave it to him. I'd never fucked anyone as hard, as deep, as brutally as I fucked Desmond. My thighs slapped against his meaty glutes, a sound I wasn't used to hearing. I was pummeling ass with my entire dick, and I was fuckin' loving it.

And so was Officer Desmond. He was actually sobbing, or maybe that was the wet juicy sound his ass was making as I forced it open to take the ravaging I was giving it. His sphincter no longer gripped my shaft, instead yielding to my drilling.

"Oh jeezus! I'm gonna fuckin' cum!" I gasped.

"Yeah, do it! Fuckin' breed me."

I grabbed his shoulders tight, half-hoisting my body onto Desmond's woolly back, and rabbit-fucked him fast and deep until my balls gave up their load. I bellowed and bucked and shook. I clawed and clutched his hairy shoulders. I screamed curse words. I came until I couldn't come any more.

When I finished planting my seed deep inside him, I examined the damage I'd done Desmond's law-enforcement ass. His butthole was a disaster area. It was red, raw, gaping, pulsing, dripping sperm and ass-juice, the hairy glutes matted with the outpouring. I gently tongued the savaged anus, and when Desmond whimpered with pleasure, I cleaned him thoroughly, inside and out, savoring the flavors.

When he couldn't take it anymore, Desmond pulled away. "Jeezus god, that was good."

"Damn right it was. But you haven't gotten off yet."

The cop saw where my gaze was focused and put his hands over his jockstrapped crotch.

"That's okay. I'll take care of myself later."

"The fuck you will, Patrick. You're gonna take care of yourself right here and now. My ass is yours, big guy, and I want you to fuck me."

The cop had a puzzled look on his face. "Wait. How'd you know my name is Patrick?"

"I went to Manning High."

"Oh jeezus god," he moaned. "So you know . . ?"

"Yeah. I know all about you."

"And you knew this before we … ?"

I nodded again. "Yeah. And you're even better than before." I looked directly at his jockstrapped crotch. "But some things don't change."

Desmond laughed nervously. "So you know what I'm packing. And that I've never gotten it inside anyone."

"Yeah. And I don't fuckin' care." I lay down and exposed my hole. "Fuck me, Patrick."

A smile crept onto his face. "Okay. All right. You asked for it. Gonna give it to you as good as I can."

He peeled off the jockstrap and towered over me, naked. His stiff dick barely protruded from his pubes, too short to extend beyond a scrotum the size of a golf ball. It was the tiniest package I'd ever seen on a grown man, and it looked even smaller on his huge body.

He knelt between my legs, his crotch against my butt, directing his tiny dick toward my willing hole. But whenever he pushed forward to penetrate me, his nutsac interfered. Occasionally he'd get his ballbag far enough out of the way and his cranberry-sized cockhead would bump against my anus, but he never actually penetrated me. He bucked and grunted and whimpered with a combination of desire, pleasure, and frustration. His hand moved rapidly and his breathing got faster.

"Yeah, fuck me, man," I said, knowing that he'd abandoned any attempt to actually do that and was literally going through the motions. "You're a damn good fucker. Gimme that fuckin' load."

He was a big-time leaker, his pre-cum glistening like dew in his red pubes. Patrick jiggled his penis with his thumb and forefinger while I dirty-talked him toward orgasm, and when he got there he bellowed as a torrent of jism spurted out of his dicklet. I was astounded at the amount of man-juice that he produced, half a dozen rope-like jets that he aimed directly at my cock and balls and butthole. He shuddered as he squeezed out the final drops, dropping to his knees and lapping up the spillage and saving it in his mouth.

He hovered above me and let the liquid dribble into my mouth, lowering his face to mine until our lips touched and we shared his jism. It was strong and pungent, salty and sour. We clutched each other tight, rolling around on the patio until we'd devoured his load.

When we pulled apart, he mumbled, "Fuckin' hot man."

"Yeah, you are."

Patrick's gaze followed mine as I looked down his body to where his dense pubes completely concealed his genitals — the reason why he'd been dubbed "Dickless Desmond." And the reason why I'd wanted him so badly.

This time he didn't stop me as I reached for his crotch. "I still want to suck you off."

"Jeezus."

Patrick rolled onto his back and locked his hands behind his head. Strong sweat scent wafted up from his pits. Sex-smell emanated from his sticky pubes. I fumbled in the jungle of hair until I finally located the lump of flesh hidden deep within. It started hardening. Desmond's green eyes bored into mine.

"Blow me."

***Jared Bascomb** is a mild-mannered civil servant who has unleashed his inner pornmaster. His stories have appeared in* Inches, Honcho, 100% Beef, *and* Handjobs *magazines. He is still working on a gay-themed mystery novel.*

Feeding

Simon Sheppard

I like to talk in bed — before, during, and after sex. And I like to have sex with big guys. So it was no surprise, at least to me, that husky Keith and I were having a conversation in the middle of a rather intense Saturday afternoon of sometimes-kinky sex.

I'd just finished sucking his cock while stroking his sizable, furry belly, taking him down my throat, backing off when he seemed like he was close to coming. Now we were lying there side by side, our hands on each other's hard dicks. He lifted up his free hand so I could bury my face in his hairy, sweaty pit, something I'd e-mailed him that I liked to do. I took a nice, deep breath of his unwashed smell. That was so nice that I felt suddenly close to coming myself. I backed away from his bushy armpit, still inhaling the scent he'd left on my face.

I was feeling in a complimentary mood. "God, you stink good," I said.

"I held off showering for three days. I'm glad I work for myself." Keith smiled an ingratiating grin.

That made me even more prone to flatter him. "And fuck, I love the combo of your big belly and small dick," I said.

"Well, thanks." His grip on my cock was absolutely superb; the guy was a jack-off expert. "I can't take credit for the size of my dick; it came as original equipment. I'm trying to lose weight, though."

I didn't know what to say to that. I liked him fine, after all, just as he was. But if he was unhappy that way, who was I to argue? Only some stranger who'd been sucking his cock a minute ago.

And, well…I hate to go there — it's the kind of thing you can't say too loudly, or even let yourself think — but part of me often wonders whether being overweight is all that healthy. Yeah, I know about the studies that show that fitness, rather than just weight, is the …

"… right?"

Whoops. Hadn't been listening. "Huh?" I replied.

Keith smiled. "Too much poppers?"

"Just enough, actually. But sorry, missed what you were saying."

"I said that I've lost over sixty pounds so far, but it's all good, right?"

"Sure." I reached for his poppers, took another hit, and, rushing like crazy, went down on his small, hard, very lovely cock. When the poppers haze cleared, I found myself stroking his big belly again, then hesitated, then stroked some more.

"I've got to pee," Keith said, sounding apologetic, "bad."

I have been known to get into water sports, but usually as a top, and that night I wasn't really in the mood to get wet. I watched Keith pad off to his bathroom. His big, hairy butt looked great; I was going to want to spank it some more when he got back.

I looked around Keith's sparsely decorated room: an indifferent smattering of books, a shelf full of DVDs, a few teddy bears lined up on a shelf, a photo of him and what had to be his parents, another picture of some guy and him, back when he weighed a lot more.

By the time Keith returned, we were in an even chattier mood, maybe because we were both thoroughly baked. Thoorouughly.

"So before you went to piss, you were saying?"

"I was, um, about to tell you about my ex." Most guys, I guess, would have found that a buzz kill.

I'm not most people. "Come back to bed," I said. "And tell me."

He lay down by my side, lifted his near arm so I could smell his musk, and guided my hand back onto his small dick. I squeezed out one last drop of pee and brought it to my lips. Sweet.

Keith's little cock was fully hard again now, standing up against the furry mound of his belly. I leaned down and took it into my mouth, a nice hot mouthful.

"My ex-boyfriend was a feeder."

I'd heard about feeders, but never met anyone who'd been involved with one. I was intrigued — though not intrigued enough to stop my cocksucking.

"He liked me to gain weight. He'd prepare high-calorie meals and tell me to eat four or five desserts. And because I loved him, I did as he said."

I thought back to my Jewish grandmother saying, "Eat! Eat! You're so skinny!" It was, I now realized, both a sign of her caring about me and a means of asserting control. I sucked even harder.

"The more I weighed," Keith continued, "the more he wanted me. He would lie there stroking my growing belly, telling me how beautiful it was. How beautiful *I* was. Wow, that feels good. Back off, or I'm going to come."

I took my mouth off his dick. "Can't have that, can we?" I scooted back up and kissed him on his very pretty mouth, his beard feeling prickly against my face. His tongue filled my mouth.

"So what happened?" I asked him when the mouth-to-mouth had ended.

"Let me suck your cock for while," Keith said, "and then I'll tell you."

I laid back, my cock — bigger and thicker than his — sticking up in the air. He hunkered down between my outspread legs and buried his face in my crotch, engulfing my cock as he did. It felt really, really good; Keith was, among other things, highly skilled at fellatio. I leaned over and stroked his meaty, hairy shoulders. At my touch, he took the head of my cock all the way down his wide-open throat. Leaning back again, I thrust upward, jamming my dick into his mouth, Moaning, Keith humped the mattress, his big, hairy ass bobbing up and down.

"Well, I love your body," I said, though I was unsure whether it was to reassure him or myself.

After a few more minutes of enthusiastic cocksucking, Keith surfaced for air. "Want another hit?" he asked, his lips wet with spit.

I nodded, and he sprang up, sitting on his haunches. "I think there's still something left in there," he said, gesturing to the bong on the bedside table.

I looked at him, sitting there looking back at me. My gaze slipped down to his stiff little cock, springing upward below his bulging belly, between his meaty thighs. I looked closely at the details of his dick — the curve, the veins, the shape of the head, the little wet pearl at the slit. *God, I love cock,* I thought. Now, I have to confess that I don't love cum so much, but Keith did, enough for both of us. He'd already made that clear, describing himself as a hungry cum-whore who craved the taste of semen. Well, he would know …

I reached over for the bong, lit it, and, listening to its comforting burble, took a big hit. As I held in the smoke, Keith spit on his hand and reached for my dick. Then, still jacking me off, he leaned over and put his mouth to mine while I exhaled.

Romantic.

"So you were telling me about your boyfriend?" This was turning into something midway between "tricking" and "therapy session," but that was okay with me.

Keith let go of my dick, took the bong, got a nice hit himself, and smiled. "Yeah. Go down on me, okay?"

He lay back on the bed and I went to work. I kissed him on the lips, then trailed my tongue over the fur of his chest, detouring sideways to one of his big nipples, taking it in my mouth and sucking like a hungry baby.

"You can bite down harder," Keith said. So I did. But nipple play always seems more interesting on the receiving end — at least to me — and I soon got bored. I let the meaty tit slip out of my mouth and revisited his smelly armpit, licking the fragrant thicket until the coarse hair was sopping wet and thoroughly matted down. Then I moved my probing mouth to his belly, kissing its convex curves, sticking the tip of my tongue in his navel. "That tickles," Keith said, with a stoned giggle.

"Of course it does," I replied. I moved down over the descending arc of Keith's belly, burying my face in his gratifyingly bushy pubes — shaving down there always seems like *such* a bad idea to me. Avoiding his hard little shaft for the moment, I licked my way down to his balls, licking on the furry sac, then taking one sizable nut in my mouth and sucking on it gently until Keith moaned.

Releasing his ball from my mouth, I licked my way down his hairy ridge till I got to his hot, furry hole. Now, I know that eating ass is stupid. I once got a torturous case of shigellosis that way. Nevertheless …

As my lips made contact with his asshole, Keith obligingly raised his knees to give me easier access. I licked the puckered flesh, flicking my tongue up and down over the ring.

"Oh fucking yeah," Keith said.

I tongued my way deeper inside, and felt him open up for me. Backing up a bit, I used my thumbs to open his hole until I saw soft, pink flesh, then dived back inside, as far in as I could get. I wanted — I *needed* — to taste his guts, consequences be damned. Where do these erotic obsessions come from? No idea. Sure, I was thoroughly stoned, but at that moment there was nothing in the world except my mouth and his hole. Nothing.

Nothing.

I have no idea how long I ate his ass that day. I only know it wasn't long enough. Not nearly long enough.

But finally Keith said, "My ass can't take much more of this, amazing as it is. I think it's time for you to come in my mouth."

I wasn't sure about that, but I had to admit to myself, if I were being honest, that my jaws were getting tired. I'd started playing with his cock while I rimmed him. Now I took both my hand and mouth away.

"Spank you first?" I asked, all horny politeness.

"Sure. Spank me during, if you want."

We rearranged ourselves again till Keith was on his belly, feeding on my dick, and his big, meaty ass was poised upward, within striking distance of my right hand. Keith pulled his lips back a little, till he was nursing hard on the tip of my hard cock. I brought my hand resoundingly down on his fleshy butt. And then again. I looked down. Pink was rising, visible through the fur. Keith's wet mouth hungrily engulfed my entire prick. I swatted him a couple more times, until he looked up and said, "Sorry, but I 'm beginning to find that distracting, when all I want to do right now is suck out all your cum. Maybe you should just fuck my face? Hard?"

"Sure thing."

So Keith got on his back, and I kneeled to either side of his big body, leaned on the headboard, and shoved my hard-on into his wide-open mouth. I started doing push-ups over him, ramming my cock all the way down his wet throat.

"Hughuh," Keith moaned.

I drew out my dick. "What?"

"Harder."

So I thrust as hard as I could, wondering how many calories I was burning. I often find it an anti-aphrodisiac to measure up to a bottom's demands, so I was feeling my orgasm recede. I was getting fatigued, too, and I figured it was time to bring things to a gooey close.

I decided to get kinky, at least in my imagination. I closed my eyes and fantasized a big muscle stud kneeling over Keith with a heavily loaded plate of food in his hand. The stud was spooning big globs of chocolate pudding and mashed potatoes into Keith's mouth. Keith, sputtering and choking, did his best to keep up with the feeding, but eventually the food overflowed his mouth, running down his bearded chin, spattering his hairy chest. Just when imaginary-Keith started to gag, I felt my cum rising.

"I'm gonna ..."

And then I shot off, straight down Keith's throat. I wish I could say it was the best orgasm of my life, but it wasn't even close — more blessed relief than star-spangled climax.

After a minute, I pulled away from Keith and rolled over on my back, landing next to him.

Keith licked his lips and said, "Yummy, that was great!"

"Glad to oblige. You want to come, too?"

"Irrelevant for me." He was playing with himself, yes, but in a leisurely, even absent-minded way, so I took him at his word.

"You were asking about my ex-boyfriend?" His voice sounded jaunty, but the look in his eyes seemed distant.

"If you want to tell me."

"Well, I discovered I was pre-diabetic." That explained the sweetness of his pee. And my grandma had been diabetic, so I knew it was no laughing matter. "I told Todd that I wanted to lose some weight, and he looked at me like I was a stranger. I loved him, I really did, but I couldn't risk losing my feet in order to make him happy. So I went on a diet. But every time I turned down dessert, it resulted in a fight." Now he sounded like he might cry, but I wasn't about to stop him from telling me the story. I reached over and rested my hand on his belly. For the first time, I looked closely and noticed the stretch marks. I leaned over and kissed him gently on the lips. His mouth tasted like jism and pot.

"So I stuck with it, and when I had lost maybe 20 or 30 pounds, I sensed he had totally lost interest in me, sexually."

"Tough one."

"It is what it is."

I suddenly wanted his cum in my mouth. Badly.

"Okay if I suck you off?"

"Sure, go for it."

It was a pleasure to put my lips back around his hard dick, to flick my tongue on its underside, taste the precum oozing from the slit. I deep-throated the smallish shaft, then backed off and gave all my attention to his swollen dickhead.

"Feels great."

Encouraged, I speeded up my sucking. Keith began thrusting his big torso upward, his thighs trembling, his breath coming fast. And then he came, a salty-sweet river flowing onto my tongue.

But Keith hadn't finished his story yet. Barely missing a breath, he continued, "Finally he left me, just left me. That was six months ago."

"I'm sorry." My mouth was tangy with the aftertaste of his cum.

"Want to know something? Part of me really regrets that I couldn't be what Todd wanted."

"Well, people are complicated." *That* was an understatement.

"I've lost a bunch more weight since then. And I'm feeling better. Hey, sorry if I burdened you with my drama."

"No problem," I said, and it wasn't. "Sometimes it's easier to confide in strangers." And to suck them off.

Keith squeezed my nipple. "Hey, he said, "you hungry? I got the munchies."

"Yeah, I could do with a snack."

Keith smiled a stoned, post-orgasmic grin. "Well, I have some butter pecan ice cream in the freezer."

"Great," I said. "Let's eat."

***Simon Sheppard** is the author of* Hotter Than Hell and Other Stories; Kinkorama: Dispatches From the Front Lines of Perversion; In Deep: Erotic Stories; *and* Sex Parties 101, *and editor of the Lammy-winning* Homosex: Sixty Years of Gay Erotica, *and of* Leathermen. *His work has also appeared in over 300 anthologies, and he writes the online serial "The Dirty Boys Club." He hangs out hirsutely at <www.simonsheppard.com>.*

Bears Write Bare

Jay Neal

I was just finishing my unpacking — unpacking doesn't take long when it's just two swimming suits and a pair of socks — when my attention was attracted by a knock on the screen door of my cabin.

"But soft! What fur through yonder screen door breaks? It is a bear and that bear is naked. Hey Magnus, come on in."

The screen door flew open and Magnus blew in like a Viking invasion. He picked me up, giving me a generous welcome kiss and a big Viking bear hug. Big Viking bear hugs are so much better when the big Viking bear is naked: fur on the back improves the grip.

"It's great to see you again, Dennis. It's been way too long. Welcome to 'The Hose'."

"It's great to be here. The place is looking great."

"And getting better all the time. We still have a lot of work to do but we wanted to have this workshop before the weather turned too cold. I'm glad you could join us."

"How could I pass up something called 'Bears Write Bare'? But what ever gave you the idea for a bear writers' camp?"

"You write. We're all bears and we're all camp! What could be more natural?"

"It's a great idea."

We'll be a cozy but interesting bunch. Five writers are attending, including you, but not to mention Thad, your workshop leader for the weekend."

"I can't wait to get started. I've got my pen, plenty of ink, and plenty of paper."

"And way too many clothes on. Why aren't you naked yet and poolside, soaking up the sun?"

"I was just unpacking."

"What's to unpack? You knew this was a clothing-*very*-optional weekend."

"Therefore I brought only the minimum: bathing suits …"

"For swimming? But —"

"For sunning. Tan lines are sexy."

"And?"

"And socks."

Magnus raised a questioning eyebrow. "To protect your modesty?"

"For sleeping," I explained, "in case the evenings are cool. I can't sleep with cold feet."

"Well, don't let cold feet keep you from the welcome picnic — maybe you'll find a bed warmer. More fun than socks."

"Speaking of bed warmers, how's Angus?"

"Speaking of picnic, he's up at the house preparing his secret family recipe for haggis. He insists on it for festive occasions."

"What's the secret?"

"That it actually tastes good!"

Our culinary conversation was cut short by the sound of a car driving up the gravel road in front of the cabins. Magnus glanced around in time to see the tail end of the car go by.

"Oh, speak of the bear, I think that was Thad's car. You'll like Thad. Western novels are his specialty. He likes his cowboys butch and horny. You two should get on just fine — unless you've got a thing against spray cheese. I'll just go and get him settled in and we'll see more of you in a little bit by the pool. Naked!"

Before I could even react the screen door banged shut with Magnus on the other side. I decided that a peek at the cowboy writer couldn't hurt so I pushed open the screen door and stepped out onto my cabin's porch.

The car had parked in front of the cabin next door. I was just in time to see Magnus giving his familiar big Viking bear greeting to the equally hefty cowboy bear as he got out of his tiny hybrid. Was it just the diminutive car that made him look big? No, definitely not. It looked like Thad was picking Magnus up and kissing him.

Conversation between the naked and the still clothed was animated. Despite the clothing, however, I was perfectly able to admire Thad's callipygian backside when he bent over the open tail-door of his car to lift out two cardboard boxes labeled CAUTION: CONTENTS UNDER PRESSURE. These he carried into his cabin.

As Thad went in, Magnus looked over at me and made a spraying motion with his finger. I couldn't remember whether I'd ever actually tasted spray cheese before. Was it really edible?

I made it to the pool within the half hour. Stripping down doesn't take long and clothing-optional wardrobe decisions are settled quickly. I went with the hunter-green suit for sunning, to bring out my coloring. I was still pale from a summer of too much daytime, indoor writing.

It was quiet poolside when I got there. Evidently I was an early arrival for the workshop. I thought the drive down from Baltimore would take longer than it had.

The sun was high, bright, and unusually hot for September. I decided to get my sunning out of the way first — precisely 27 minutes each, front and back, or else I burn like a lobster and end up covered in freckles. The first side is always pleasant, but by the time I turn over on my stomach I'm usually getting bored.

That's a good time to work out plot twists in whatever I'm working on at the moment. Right then it was the fourth book in my Miss Mindy the Detecting Librarian series. Even as I lay soaking up the sun, Miss Mindy was trying to escape the evil clutches of a nefarious bookbinder by cracking a secret message coded in Library-of-Congress call numbers. Tricky.

Fortunately (for me, not for Miss Mindy), by the time I turned over to my stomach there was some activity to distract me. On the patio deck a few steps above pool level, Magnus and Angus were moving around amongst the picnic tables, making preparations for the welcome picnic.

After a bit Thad showed up on the patio. He sat at one of the tables, talking with our hosts. Once again his admirable backside was presented for my delectation, but naked this time. He was sitting in the shade but after awhile I was able to make out the lovely pattern of fur as it swirled into the crack of his ass cheeks. It was providential that I was lying on my stomach at the time, although the distraction meant that Miss Mindy would remain imperiled that much longer.

Sometime in the other four workshop participants all showed up and made their way into the pool. By the time I was done sunning and ready for a dip they had all introduced themselves and were bobbing together in a small conversational group.

It seemed strange for me to be taking off my swimming suit to get in the pool, but that was the protocol. My skin was already getting a little crispy from the sun so I was happy I had worn something to protect my delicate bits. The water felt cold when I first slipped in but it was comfortable after only a few seconds. Have you ever noticed how much more relaxing a swimming pool can be if you're naked?

I bobbed over to join the conversation. The others had become well rehearsed with their introductions by then, so that was briskly dispensed with. Starting from my left:

- *Ramon:* dark hair, trim mustache, mischievous eyes. Writes artistic, broody novels for satisfaction, romance novels under a pseudonym to pay the bills.
- *Philip:* tall and hefty with a big belly, short salt and pepper hair all over and a long beard to match. Had surprisingly large nipples. Writes poetry, mostly pornographic sonnets, but has been working on something epic in Alexandrine couplets. He and Ramon have been partners for 19 years; they got married in Canada two years ago.
- *Myron:* short, mousy hair, on the thin side but very hairy, notably on his knuckles and wrists. Writes short stories filled with suburban Jewish gay angst, often in Yiddish.
- *Kevin:* fireplug build, shaved head, multiple piercings with large-gauge rings, multiple tattoos — it looked like a peacock on his back but only the tip of the tail was above water, so I couldn't be sure. Writes screenplays for independent horror films and hardcore S/M videos.

Our conversation was light and inconsequential and ran along predictable lines: weather, recipes, and men. Being writers we talked about everything except writing. However much we might deny it, we writers love to hear other people praise our work but, secretly, we really believe that everyone actually hates our writing and we're afraid of rejection so we tend to avoid the topic. It's a lot like dating that way.

And, of course, we talked about Thad.

Ramon: "He's got nice hands. They remind me of Hemingway's hands. I always key on the hands for some reason."

Philip: "I've read a couple of his books. His writing is very lyrical and the characterization of the horses is surprisingly good."

Myron: "Flattop haircuts are so sixties. It looks good on him. With the very contemporary, bushy schnauzer beard, his look's hot."

Kevin: "He's got a great ass. I wonder what his asshole tastes like?"

Thad was now sitting back against his table facing the pool, eyes closed, catching some rays. A can of spray cheese was on the table beside him. We obviously didn't have to waste time speculating on the size of his schlong since its majesty was quite evident for all to see. While I was watching — not staring, just glancing discreetly — Thad grabbed the can of spray cheese, put the nipple in his mouth, and took a hit. Odd.

"What's his thing with the spray cheese?" I asked the group. No one offered any theories, but Myron did say he thought it was "hot."

My reverie was interrupted by the sound of a very large gong and Magnus' voice announcing: "Cocktails! Everyone out of the pool for cocktails!" I'd never realized what a funny word "cocktails" was in a clothing optional context.

We started moving toward the ladder at the side of the pool. Kevin said, "You guys go ahead. I can't get out yet."

I'm sure I looked confused. Ramon nodded pointedly into the water in Kevin's direction and stage whispered, "Erection difficulties."

"More like a distinct lack of erection difficulties, I'd say," Philip said.

Myron bobbed over behind Kevin's back and snuggled up close, reaching his arms around Kevin's belly. "Here, I'll help."

"I'm not sure that's helping," Kevin said.

"It will," Myron said.

The welcome picnic had broken up about an hour earlier and I was sitting in the rocking chair on my cabin's porch, enjoying the sounds of the evening. The party was fun, but you wouldn't expect less from Magnus and Angus. For cocktails Magnus served potent Cosmopolitans — red — and some blue concoction of vodka and blue Curaçao. They certainly lubricated the proceedings.

If I hadn't tasted it myself I wouldn't have believed it, but Angus's secret family haggis recipe really was good. It ran a close second in popularity behind the grilled hot dogs, which took on a vaguely suggestive quality in the clothing-optional context.

We all got to know Thad better. Ramon seemed mostly fixated on Thad's hands while Philip wanted to talk about homoeroticism in cowboy poetry. Myron was far more obvious than he thought he was staring at Thad's crew cut; the way Myron kept brushing his hand over the top of his own head only drew more attention to it. I was convinced that Kevin was trying to think of a pretext for sniffing Thad's ass, but he never managed it.

Depending on your point of view, I had been fortunate or unfortunate enough to sit next to Thad while we ate. I had been so aware of his proximity I thought I could have counted the hairs on his thighs where it pressed against mine. I had been certain I could feel the heat radiating from his body, although it could have been my incipient sunburn. Once he had dropped some potato salad in my lap. I had rather hoped — and was mortified at the thought — that he would offer to lick it off.

Thad's habit of taking occasional hits from his can of spray cheese was inexplicably becoming erotically charged for me. The way he had sprayed it along his hot dog was so arousing that I feared I'd have to stay seated at the picnic table long after dinner had ended because of "erection difficulties." But I hadn't and the picnic had drawn to a decorous close.

It was a lot darker in the wilds of Croom than it ever could have been at home in Baltimore. A lot quieter, too, although all the crickets and frogs made quite a racket. Still, I could hear the faint buzzing of the neon sign that proclaimed the "White Ho se Motor Inn." Magnus had explained at dinner that no one seemed to know whether the missing neon letter had been a "u" or "r," so they had compromised and called it "The White Hose." Someday, when they could afford a new sign, Magnus said they would be changing the name to "Bear Woods."

Here's another difference between Croom and Baltimore. I'd never been inclined to sit on the front stoop of my row house almost naked — or totally naked, if I kicked off my flip-flops.

The vital feature of this porch, of course, was that I could observe Thad's cabin from it. All coming and goings, of which there had been none to that point, were revealed to me. Unless he had come back right after dinner and went to bed early. But how likely was that? Surely an evening like that was quality time for lonesome cowboys to sit in the moonlight by the fire, strumming their mistuned guitars and working out another verse of their homoerotic cowboy poetry.

Thoughts of poking cows made me restless, so I decided on a moonlit stroll before bedtime. Maybe I'd work on a cowboy ballad of my own.

I took the gravel road up the hill toward the main house, behind which was the patio deck and the pool. Coincidentally, that was the route that took me past Thad's cabin, so I could casually check that all of his lights really were off. Perhaps, if he were in bed, I'd hear his snoring. I briefly thought maybe I'd catch a glimpse of him sleeping in the buff though an open window, until I remembered that there really was no point since I had spent a good part of the afternoon gazing upon his naked glory. Still, it was a nice thought.

Even plain, ordinary gray gravel looked curiously opalescent in full moonlight. Isn't that odd? Maybe my mind was playing tricks. Maybe I had too many blue cocktails at dinner. As I approached the house, which was dark, I imagined I heard a distant wind, rustling in the trees, but I could see that no wind was stirring. Perhaps it was more like the sound of air escaping a bicycle tire?

In reality, as I turned the corner and came around to the patio deck, I could see that the sound was much more like the jets in a hot tub. In fact, like the jets in a hot-tub swirling water around the semi-recumbent figure of Thad. His head was leaning back; his eyes were closed. I felt strangely reassured to see a can of spray cheese close at hand.

He cracked open an eyelid. "Hey there, pa'dner. Why don't you come on in and sit a spell?"

"Are we going to sing cowboy songs?"

"I 'spect we could rustle us up a few. Did you bring your guitar?"

"Tarnation! I left it in my saddlebag."

"Ah, well. Left to our own devices then. How's your *a capella* singing?"

I kicked off my flip-flops and began the inelegant task of getting into the hot tub.

"No worse than my accompanied singing."

"That bad, is it?"

It's difficult to sit in a hot tub with someone of Thad's commanding presence, not to mention imposing bulk, without some part of one person's person touching some part of the other person's person. Since our thighs were already well acquainted I settled on sitting next to him, our legs stretched out in parallel. For his part Thad was willing to put his arm around my shoulder when I slumped down into the water. It created the potential for cozy cowboy conversation.

"My singing ability is probably the best argument in favor of my being a writer," I explained.

We hadn't discussed writing at dinner, so Thad asked me about mine. I told him about Miss Mindy and her current troubles. Thad told me about some of his cowboys and their affairs of the heart and how big cattle drives and long hours in their saddles wearing the same sweaty, smelly clothing made the cowboys really, really horny.

Our conversation wandered aimlessly yet amicably as we watched the nearly full moon drift across the sky. As our conversation became more personal, I found myself snuggling a little closer to Thad until I was comfortably nestled against his chest, his arm draped casually over my left shoulder. When he turned his head occasionally in my direction, his beard tickled the top of my head. Many cowboy secrets were shared, but one question remained.

"So what's up with the spray-cheese thing?" I asked.

"It keeps me off the pork rinds."

"Pork rinds?"

"They give me the runs something awful."

"I guess that's a benefit then."

"I figure it's also a subconscious acknowledgment of my obsessive lust for men with red hair."

"Really!"

"Of course, there's also the obvious aspect of oral gratification."

"But I have red hair."

"I am aware of that fact, although I'd describe it more as light coppery with overtones of pomegranate."

He kissed the top of my head. It tickled. He also pinched my left nipple. That was much better than a mere tickle, sort of a full-body tickle.

Thad was evidently talking — I heard the rumble in his chest — but I hadn't been paying much attention. Blame it on the nipple tweak that had transferred all thought processes to the little brain in my crotch.

"I'm sorry, what were you saying? I was distracted by the inviting sight of the watery effervescence swirling just below your nipple."

"Nothing important, obviously. But with an invitation like that, perhaps you should RSVP with some alacrity."

I did. My chin was already skimming the water, my tongue conveniently at nipple level. By slipping my arm across the broad expanse of Thad's belly, I turned just enough to bring my lips into contact with the target nipple. I licked, bit gently, and sucked lightly, making sounds that syncopated nicely with the sucking sound of the water lapping in the hot-tub filters.

Thad moaned. You might think that writers would be more creatively articulate at such times, but you would be mistaken. Apparently the little brain has a very limited vocabulary.

My arm across Thad's belly had a hand that was unoccupied, so I reached up and gave a pinch and a little twist to his other nipple. Like a volume knob, it turned up his moaning. We still were not louder than the frogs though.

Both nipples were well hardened and Thad's volume was adjusted perfectly, so I disengaged from nipple sucking and raised my head to enjoy some good, old-fashioned cowboy kissing. I have always enjoyed a little beard burn around the mouth. I quickly discovered that Thad had a long and muscular tongue, which he used to explore the inside of my cheeks.

Meanwhile I let my free arm slide back down his belly and under the water until my hand encountered his stiff dick. Erection difficulties indeed! The warm water had loosened his balls; they floated playfully around my hand so I played with them for a minute or two while Thad's little moans made my lips vibrate. Then I wrapped my fingers as far around his dick as they could reach and stroked slowly, ever so slowly. My lips vibrated even more.

Thad stopped kissing me and pulled me closer to him. He whispered in my ear, "I think Magnus discourages sex in the hot tub. It tends to clog the filters."

"Maybe if I do it slowly enough it isn't sex."

"I think that sooner or later it's going to be sex regardless of speed."

I continued my measured stroking of Thad's dick and my attempts at mouth-to-mouth beard abrasion. My ministrations were effective. Thad kept clenching me ever more tightly against his body until it was becoming difficult to breath, but I wasn't about to complain — what a way to go! Thad was approaching his own *petite mort*, evidenced by uncontrollable shuddering as all his muscles tensed.

Through barely moving lips he managed to say, "It's about to be sex."

I was seized by inspiration of the moment. I broke my clench with Thad, took a deep breath, and plunged my head under the water. My beard-burned lips made a good seal that I could slide slowly down Thad's dick. The result was a mouthful of Thad rather than a mouthful of water.

Sucking him into my mouth was just enough to send him over the edge. Happily, with my head under water, Thad's very loud orgasmic howling was muffled. He thrashed about, howling and slapping the water in a very gratifying way. He also came copiously in my mouth — cum that would not be clogging the hot-tub filters, I might add.

As soon as I could I came up for air, gasping and swallowing. After a bit Thad pulled me back against him and I snuggled up to his chest again. He murmured something like, "Git along, little doggie."

Thad took a hit of spray cheese, then he squirted a warm, creamy shot in my mouth. It was very romantic. We sat quietly in the warm, bubbling water, turning into cowboy prunes together as the moon arced gracefully across the sky.

I slept very well, thank you. I didn't have to get up early either. Angus served a lovely late-morning brunch of scrambled eggs, Canadian bacon, a startlingly good grits casserole, and homemade muffins featuring various berries. The program for the day was brunch then mid-day workshop session, afternoon snacks, lounging-by-the-pool time, and an evening session after dinner.

Our midday session was going to deal with "Plot Problems and Narrative Disasters," things all writers faced. We lounged around on the picnic tables, Thad at the center of our semicircle. We looked casual in our birthday suits but we were all intensely interested in the topic.

Ramon started things off. "I'm often concerned about how to work in physical description without sounding contrived."

"As in 'Archie turned and saw the six-foot-two-inch-tall stranger with the fifty-four-inch hairy chest and forty-two-inch waist standing naked before him, proudly showing off his eleven-inch dick'?" Thad asked. "Often your readers will be satisfied with a lot less physical description than you imagine necessary."

"True," I said. "I like to keep the details sketchy myself. Plus, quite a bit of description can be accomplished indirectly."

Thad took a hit of spray cheese.

"Exactly," Ramon added. "For instance, I could simply remark on how fascinated I am by the way Thad's beautifully shaped hands flex and turn when he picks up the can of spray cheese."

"Also," Myron added, "since we've already established that he's naked, I could observe to Ramon that despite a generous flaccid endowment, I suspect that Thad's a grower." Naturally, I nodded complete agreement.

Philip looked thoughtful. "That's all useful, but I think the real challenge is how to get the sex scene rolling without succumbing to tired old formulae."

"In real life," Myron asked, "how often have we actually heard someone say 'I was so drunk last night ...'?"

"Once, maybe," Kevin said, "but I was too hung over to remember the details."

"On the other hand," Myron said, "who among us has not lusted after some straight guy only to end up an emotional wreck?"

There were lots of nods. Thad offered his advice: "Let the sex scenes grow naturally from the narrative context and the characters' emotions and established behavior. You probably will have some telling details lying around in your story not pulling their own weight. Grab one of those and turn it into a plot device."

Thad took another hit of spray cheese.

Kevin got visibly excited. "You mean something like the spray cheese, for instance?"

Philip looked puzzled. "I'm afraid I don't see how that would work."

"O ye of little imagination," Kevin intoned. "Look, if you've got a bunch of naked guys sitting around and an open can of spray cheese nearby, you just know that sooner or later it's going to get sprayed up someone's ass."

Philip seemed startled by the idea. "Really? That doesn't sound terribly plausible to me."

"Oh," Myron said, "I think it sounds eminently plausible. It sounds like a lot of fun, too!"

Myron jumped up from his table and pointed enquiringly at the can of spray cheese, which Thad handed to him. Myron turned toward Kevin and spread his arms in invitation.

Kevin hardly needed to be asked twice. He hopped up onto his table, rolled onto his back, lifted his legs, and used both hands to spread his cheeks. Myron stuck the nipple of the spray-cheese can into Kevin's receptive asshole and sprayed, ultimately pulling it out and making a little rosette to cap Kevin's hole. He set the can on the table, sat himself down for a feast, and began licking off the cheese he had so adroitly deployed.

"Aw, fuck man!" Kevin was clearly enjoying this plot device. "Fuck! That feels so good. Do you think spray cheese would make good lube?"

"It's undoubtedly slippery enough," Myron said, "but almost certainly not condom friendly."

"Aw, fuck! Use your fingers then."

"How many?"

"All of them!"

Philip observed this demonstration by Kevin and Myron with great interest. "I think I'm beginning to see," he said. Ramon was certainly catching on since he, like the rest of us by that time, was experiencing serious erection difficulties. Armed with newfound comprehension, Philip fetched the can of spray cheese and spritzed out a sinuous cheese-snake along the entire length of Ramon's hard dick.

"Hot dog!" Philip exclaimed with evident delight at his own witticism.

"Don't you think," Ramon asked, "that the hot-dog imagery is rather clichéd?"

"Clichéd, perhaps, but of great utility and singularly appropriate at this moment." Philip squatted in front of Ramon. "I'll eat it here, thank you, and save the buns 'til later." He bent forward and sucked Ramon's entire dick into his mouth, undertaking a vigorous, if cheesy, blowjob.

I looked at Thad. Thad looked at me. He shrugged his shoulders.

"Well," I said, "the class seems to be a success so far."

"The students are certainly engaged in the topic and unusually motivated by the classroom exercises."

Thad continued his thought. "Do you suppose we should take a few minutes and review our lesson on cowboy songs from last night? I do believe I owe you a verse or two."

"It sounds like a plan to me."

Thad got up and retrieved the can of spray cheese. He stood in front of me, pondering for a moment before piping, with exaggerated care, tiny cheese flowers on each of my nipples.

"Pasties?" I asked.

"Cheesies," he responded solemnly. Then he started licking them off.

I brushed my hand over Thad's bristly flattop, enjoying all the sensations I was experiencing.

"Yee haw!" I whispered to myself. "Ride 'em cowboy."

Jay Neal *is a long-time connoisseur of bears: "husky" is his favorite flavor and he has a weakness for men best described as "big lugs." His stories have appeared in several magazines and more than a dozen anthologies. He and his partner share a life of domestic contentment near Washington, D.C.*

Hair Trigger

Dale Chase

I didn't want to kill Everett Dunn but when a fellow draws on you there's no time to reason, even if it's some hothead kid tryin to make a name knockin off Roy Weeks. So I shot him and he died then and there and I felt bad not for what I done but for what he did, gettin himself killed for nothin. It happened before, down in Tombstone, and I suppose it'll happen again because some just don't stop to think.

I shoulda left town then but I'd traveled all the way from Montana and wanted to stay put awhile. And I was enjoyin more than my share of winnin hands as there were plenty of takers for a good game, not to mention the ruffians liked keeping company with a man who washed regular and didn't look like he'd come in off the range. So I kept my room, my poker, and now and then had a good fuck from some cowhand come to town on payday. I'd take his money at the table and by the time he was clean, we both knew what was next and I'd quit then, go outside, around back, and he'd follow and it would be one rough one he'd give me but then I liked it that way, cock hard up my chute, angry cowboy fuckin me cause I'd fucked him at cards. I'd come big time while he did me, dick goin off like cannon fire while he unloaded. Then he'd pull out and I'd turn, see the grin cause now we was even. He'd lost his money but he'd had my ass.

Sometimes it wasn't a loser that did me. Sometimes I lost a bit on purpose just to let the cowboy feel good awhile. His chest would puff up, he'd sit straighter in his chair, and I'd bet his dick was hard cause he'd be passin me the eye. And when we fucked it was a whole different thing than with the losers. Winners liked to suck me off first and I'd come into their throats while they worked their dicks below. Then I'd bend, take the cock, and we'd have a good long fuck because there wasn't no anger now, just pleasure.

So I was sittin at the table with three men, well into winning, when Abram Dunn came in. I didn't know him so paid no attention but the fellow to my left nudged me, said he was the brother of the fellow I'd killed day before, and chairs scraped the floor as players deserted me. Alone at the table, I kept a hand on my gun, watchin Abram Dunn approach.

He was older than Everett and bigger, dusty from his sweat stained Stetson down to his chewed up boots. He looked like he'd been on the range for a month and maybe he had. Body was thick, woolen shirt pulled tight over the heft, pants ridin low, thick thighs. Didn't look no relation to Everett who was long and lean but the expression he wore told different. He fixed on me lookin more determined than angry and when he stood just beyond my table he said "You the one killed my brother" and I nodded.

He seemed to think on this which was good as a hothead woulda drawn right then. I offered nothing more as I like a man to think. Saves me the trouble killin him more often than not. And as this one thought, this Abram Dunn, I noted his shirt unbuttoned at the top, hair sproutin there so thick there had to be a pelt down his front and my dick stirred at such a thought cause I always like a hairy man. Somethin animal about it, some kinda throwback even though I mostly found them gentler than the others. Maybe animal kept a man sane.

"Why'd you do it?" he asked.

"Didn't want to. He drew on me before I could talk him out of it."

"You do that, talk 'em out of it?"

"Sometimes, specially if it's some kid lookin to make a name which is what I fear your brother was after."

He considered this and I noted his hand was not on his gun. The saloon was quiet, men at the bar turned away from us, those at the tables keepin to their games but all listenin, waitin, probably figurin I'd draw and kill him too. But I didn't want to kill him and from the look on his face, he didn't want to kill me neither. Pain showed more than anger and maybe confusion as to what he should do. Everyone knew a brother must avenge a killin but this man was no hothead. Must be thirty or more, I thought, around my age. Experienced at life which his brother was not so much. Maybe knowin I'd kill him if he drew.

"I ain't come to kill you," he said then. "Just to look at the kinda man who could gun down a kid who didn't know no better. He was my only brother and now he's gone cause of you and your damnable gun. I hope one day somebody kills you and you rot in hell for eternity cause that's surely where you belong."

I said nothing but could feel the stir around me as others took in what he said and I felt worse than if he'd drawn cause then we'd have ended it clean where this strung it out like some sermon gone too long. My finger slid up against the trigger cause right then I wanted to be rid of this fellow one way or t'other. My breath began to labor, my heart to pound, all the while him drillin me with those eyes that condemned more than any hangin judge.

I almost said I was sorry but that would have been wrong cause I killed in defense of myself. I was sorry the kid drew, sorry he had to die, but I wasn't gonna tell all that to the brother so I let him have his say and his quiet, and then he shook his head and left. The entire place heaved a collective sigh.

It was late afternoon and I'd been at the table most of the day so I got up, much to everyone's relief, and went outside. Not to follow Abram Dunn although I did catch sight of him crossin the street and noted how he stepped sure, no swagger. He paused before the sheriff's office, then went in, and I considered leavin town as I don't need the law on me but I also knew Sheriff Burden a fair man who knew a fair fight and figured he'd set the brother straight. So I took up a spot outside the Mercantile, had me a smoke, and in time Abram Dunn emerged and stood lookin like he had nowheres else to go.

I thought to cross to him, take him up and comfort him but how wrong would that be, killer coming to ease the wound? He'd want no part of me even as somethin about him made me want to be part of him and I honestly do not know what that somethin was. Not killin his brother. Maybe not wantin to kill his brother. Or maybe just him as he was an impressive sight, so said the stir in my crotch. But I did nothing that day, saw him get on a sorrel horse and ride away and figured that the last of it although that night lyin in my bed I abused my cock somethin fierce with thoughts of him comin at me with his dick out.

Two days later, when I figured it near time to move on, maybe back to Texas, there came Abram Dunn on his sorrel horse. I'd just had me a bath and a shave and had come outside all spiffed to get some air and there he was, gettin off his horse at the sheriff's office. Went in which bothered me as there was nothin to be done about the killin so why keep on? I went down to stand directly across so he'd see me when he come out and he did, drillin me that look again. He wore a blue shirt that day and it made his color come up ruddy like and I saw how handsome he was, not smooth like me but rugged from ranch work. I liked my men rugged and for a second I forgot what lay between us and thought only of my dick which twitched with need. I shifted my weight from foot to foot as my bottom muscle clenched in agreement. I'd let him fuck me if he wanted but he probably wouldn't want to do the man killed his brother. Still, a man's privates can get him past a whole lot.

He didn't get back on the sorrel, he started off down the street so I crossed over and followed, not sure what I was up to but goin ahead anyways. He went clear down to the stable, then turned there so I did too and he was out of sight so I kept on, down between the buildings and when I reached the back I was suddenly taken around the neck by an arm of iron which tightened and I began to choke.

I rammed an elbow back to his gut which caused him to loosen his grip and we began to struggle with one another. As with his brother, I did not wish to harm this man but he was upon me and I had no choice. Fortunately we were the same height though he had a good thirty pounds on me but I had quickness on my side and I knew a man's weak points. I landed good punches but so did he, powerful assaults to my ribs and jaw that had the strength of justification behind them.

Nobody could see us where we was, down where nobody much went, so we battled to ourselves, hands grapplin one another on the ground, dust flying, fists connecting with flesh now and again, some chokin, some knees. Never had such a fight as that. After some minutes he pinned me to the ground, face in the dirt, and he growled how I had no right to take a life, especially one so young, how I was older and should know how to avoid kids like Everett, and as he told this I heard his voice break and thought tears to be in his eyes which stopped me fightin him. And then, much to my surprise, he was on top of me, the whole of him humpin my ass. Still pinned, I felt a hard dick against me and realized what we could do so I told him he could fuck me and I bared my bottom.

I had no idea how much he had in his pants but when he put it to me, it caused my breath to catch because he had a big one and it blazed a new trail goin in. And as he began to fuck like some mad bull, I thought how maybe this was his way to get back at me, get off at the same time. Fuck me like the losers did cept he was no loser and this was way too much thinkin so I stopped that and just took his cock.

He pulled my ass high so to get in better and then he had the whole of it, goin clear up in my gut which caused my stiff dick to shoot a load into the dirt. He kept at me for some time and I admired his stayin power. Then he moaned and I knew his stuff was spurtin into me which I always liked, takin a man's spunk. He pounded on me til he was empty, then drew back and I rolled over to see his cock still up, cock more for bear than man with thick fur around the base and I wanted to get down and suck on it for I hadn't had a suck in awhile but I held off cause I didn't know what he'd do next. Then I saw he was as confused as I was, two men on opposite sides of a terrible thing, crossin over by way of their dicks and not sure the right or wrong.

He made no move to cover himself, sat there on his haunches and his thing gradually went soft but still, hanging there over a pair of fat balls, it was a sight to behold. And I wanted to tell him this but couldn't speak for loss of what would be right. If it was just sex between us, there would be much to say but with the other I had no idea. Fortunately, he did.

"I hate you for what you did to my brother," he said, "but God help me I had to have you."

I wanted to tell him he could keep on havin me but I just nodded cause he seemed to dislike what he'd done. His hand dropped to his cock and he pulled on it like it was reassurance things was still right, and I ached to help him but did nothin. So he stood and closed his pants and I did likewise and we remained opposite, paralyzed until I said "I'm sorry." I had never said that to no man. Cause I'd never been sorry before.

He shut his eyes a second, then nodded and walked away and I thought that's it and I'm leavin for Texas to forget all this. I went to the hotel, packed my bag, paid my bill, got my horse, and left town, all the while his stuff drippin outa my hole. In the saddle my bottom felt wet from him which made me think on the fuck as I walked my horse along.

Payin little attention, I kept to the road and then the hand of fate or God or some such came down upon me for there up ahead was that sorrel horse and astride it, Abram Dunn. My reaction to the sight of him told the story cause not only did my crotch give me a pleasurable start, my breath caught and I swear my heart picked up a beat. Even my horse seemed to know somethin was afoot as he raised his head and gave a shudder down his whole self but then animals know when fuckin is in the air.

Abram rode slowly yet remained tall in the saddle and I liked the sight of him from behind, broad, solid, big legs around his horse and I thought of them around me, how I'd like to get onto that body of his when he was naked, crawl around, suck his dick and maybe his tits, run my fingers into the hair that no doubt covered much of him. By the time I reached him I was stiff in my pants.

"Leavin?" he said when I rode up beside him.

"Yep. Figure I'm better off in Texas."

We rode on awhile longer before he said, "No need" which was remarkable, considerin what I'd done to him but then we had the fuck which complicated things.

"That's big of you," I said, "but I don't want to be in town for a good long time. Maybe stop playin cards, maybe get me ranch work. Used to be a right good hand."

I heard him sigh then. Out in the open you can hear a cricket sneeze and the sound of him lettin go like that moved me because he needed no words. But after awhile he managed some.

"Come work for me if you want."

I was shakin my head even as I agreed because it went against everything in the world when you've killed somebody, no matter how rightly done.

"Just up the road a piece," Abram said and so I followed him to his ranch where a fine little house sat in a grove of cottonwoods alongside a small stream. Barn and horse corrals nearby, chicken coop, dogs comin to greet us. He dismounted but I hesitated, unsure even though there we were. I'd been a gambler so long, ranch seemed foreign and there was also the possibility that all was not as he'd said. I'd never met a forgivin man, especially one sufferin such as loss as his and I found part of me wanted to console him while another stood guard.

He didn't linger but put his horse in the barn, unsaddled it, fed it, and I was left to do likewise. I then followed him into the house. The place was finer than expected, bore a woman's touch even though none was about. Curtains hung at the windows and chairs and setee were upholstered though faded some. Maybe a family place that had come down to the brothers.

Abram built a fire in the kitchen stove, set coffee to brewin. I sat at his table with no idea what to say. Besides fuckin and killin, we had little in common. And I hadn't been in a house for some time. Always put up in hotels in town so I kinda liked the quiet here, just him and me.

"I'm at a loss," I told him when he set cups of coffee before us and sat down.

He heaved a great sigh, looked into his coffee but did not drink. "I seen you some time ago, when you first got to town. Everett and me stopped for a drink and saw you playin cards and I could feel excitement on him cause he knew who you were. 'That's Roy Weeks,' he told me. 'Killed four men who cheated him at cards. Nobody faster. Look at him'

"I'd heard of you but wasn't impressed same as Everett. Cards and killin ain't much of a life to me but to a young fellow itchin for more than ranchin, you was way too big. And he'd practiced his gunplay for some time which I couldn't have discouraged even had I tried."

"I ain't killed four men," I told him.

He shrugged. "Don't matter."

"Does to me. I killed one man in Tombstone. Wounded others for dealin from the bottom. Never wanted to kill nobody, includin your brother."

"I know that. If it weren't you it'da been Jake Steed or Ralph Kerner or some other gunfighter. He knew of em all."

We drank our coffee and I relaxed some because I could see he told the truth. I also felt no revenge in him. What came over me was sadness cause he was now alone, deprived of a brother. I had no idea how I could help but to take the job he offered, get to know him, which would be good for me. And we could fuck which I knew would ease his pain and I thought to that now, sat back, undid my pants, pushed em down. My dick came up soon as I considered this. Abram still looked sad when he came around the table to kneel and get his mouth onto me, suckin so fierce I came too quick.

When he sat back and licked his lips, I asked could we undress and get to a bed and he agreed, took me to the bedroom where sat a good strong four-poster. As I stripped, I watched him shed his clothes, eager to finally see the whole of him and then there he was, big bear of a man and I grabbed my prick cause what else is a man to do in the face of such a sight?

His pelt was rich brown, same color I'd seen on a bear once, and I thought back to how the bear had roared, tellin me he owned the forest and he'd eat me sure as not. Now I had my own grizzly and if this one wanted to eat me, I'd gladly become his meal.

He pulled on his dick which was hard out and I climbed onto the bed which was welcome after so many back alley fucks. He got on and turned me onto my side, put a finger up my bottom, started to prod while his mouth nibbled my neck. I grabbed my spent cock and held on.

Then he pressed himself to me, fur against my back, while his cock slid up my crack and rubbed there some. I could tell he was working himself up to it, enjoyin the climb which I welcomed as it's some good climb. But then he flipped me onto my stomach, raised my bottom, and shoved his big piece of bear meat into me and holy God, I thought I'd pass out. Never mind it had been in me before. There was somethin new this time, maybe that things between us was settled or maybe just bein in a bed, to ourselves now, not fightin and fuckin, just fuckin.

Dale Chase *has been writing male erotica for a decade with 125 stories published in various magazines and anthologies, most recently in* Time Well Bent *from Lethe Press and* Rough Trade *from Bold Strokes Books. Chase's fiction has been translated into Italian and German and a sole literary effort appeared in the* Harrington Gay Men's Fiction Quarterly. *Chase's first collection,* If the Spirit Moves You: Ghostly Gay Erotica, *is due from Lethe Press in 2010.*

About the Editor

***R. Jackson** has edited several books of gay / bi / queer men's fiction, including the fiction anthology* Bi Guys, *a Lambda Literary Award finalist in Bisexual Literature. He also edited the anthology trilogy of* Bearotica, Bear Lust, *and* Bears in the Wild. *With P. J. Willis, Jackson coedited* Kink: Tales of the Sexual Adventurer. *Jackson's writing credits include* American Bear *and* 100% Beef *magazines; he also contributed a regular column for several months to the Daddyhunt.com blog.*

Breinigsville, PA USA
22 June 2010
240399BV00001B/20/P